Mostly Ghostly 6

Let's Get This Party Haunted!

Experience all the chills of the Mostly Ghostly series!

Mostly Ghostly 6

Let's Get This Party Haunted!

R.L. STINE

DELACORTE PRESS
A PARACHUTE PRESS BOOK

Published by
Delacorte Press
an imprint of
Random House Children's Books
a division of Random House, Inc.
New York

Visit us on the Web! www.randomhouse.com/kids
Educators and librarians, for a variety of teaching tools, visit us at
www.randomhouse.com/teachers

Library of Congress Cataloging-in-Publication Data

Stine, R.L.
Let's get this party haunted! / R.L. Stine.
p. cm. — (Mostly ghostly)
"A Parachute Press book."
Summary: Max's twelfth birthday party turns into a major disaster
when ghosts Nicky and Tara boycott it, and sinister events spin
out of control.
ISBN 0-385-74693-8 (hardcover) — ISBN 0-385-90931-4 (lib. bdg.)
[1. Ghosts—Fiction. 2. Birthdays—Fiction. 3. Parties—Fiction.
4. Horror stories.] I. Title.
PZ7.S86037Let 2005
[Fic]—dc22
2005003278

Printed in the United States of America

July 2005

10 9 8 7 6 5 4 3 2 1

1

JUGGLING DUCKPINS IS NOT as easy as it looks. The duckpins are very heavy on the bottom and light on the top. You have to remember this when you toss them up, and when you catch them.

If you give them the wrong spin, they'll come down bottom first, which is wrong. You need to grab the top of the pin and toss it up again.

I don't have a problem getting the spin right. I have two other problems. The first is that the ceiling in my bedroom is very low. So when I toss duckpins up, sometimes they hit the ceiling and then come crashing down on my head.

The second problem is that my house is haunted. I am haunted by two ghosts—kids about my age—named Nicky and Tara Roland. And believe it or not, I am the only one in my family who can see or hear them.

Why are Nicky and Tara a juggling problem?

I'll tell you.

There I was, practicing my juggling in my

room. I always start with two duckpins. To get used to the weight. Then I add a third.

I was working very hard because I wanted to be perfect. See, I was rehearsing for my birthday party. My new friend, Quentin, and I are magicians and jugglers. And we were going to perform at my twelfth birthday party.

All the cool kids from school were coming to my party. I hadn't invited them yet. But I *hoped* they'd all come. I knew they would—*if* I could convince Traci Wayne to come.

Traci is the coolest, hottest girl at Jefferson Elementary. I don't know if I'm in love with her or not. But every time I get in the same room with her, I start panting like a dog, my tongue sticks to the roof of my mouth, and all I can say is "Hunh hunh hunh."

Is that true love? I'm not sure. But I *was* sure that if Traci agreed to come to my birthday party, all her cool friends would follow her.

When you're twelve, you're almost a teenager. Which means you're not a kid anymore. You're cool, and you have to act cool all the time.

I couldn't wait to be twelve. Because so far, I hadn't been cool at all. I was not in the cool group at school. I was in the group known as Geek Patrol, the bottom of the food chain.

Which is totally unfair. Just because my best friend, Aaron, and I wear *Battlestar Galactica*

T-shirts and can recite whole *Buffy* episodes word for word—that doesn't make us geeks!

Being a great magician isn't geeky either. That's what I hoped to prove at my birthday party.

And that's what I was thinking about as I practiced my juggling. I wanted to put on a perfect show to impress Traci and all the other kids.

So I was in my room, tossing up the duckpins, just starting to get the rhythm right. Thinking about Traci Wayne and how I had to invite her ASAP.

And suddenly, all three pins froze in midair.

They stuck up there, about a foot or two above my head, and didn't come down.

Of course I knew why.

"Nicky? Tara? Give me a break," I said. "I don't have time to mess around. I'm rehearsing."

They both appeared in front of me. Nicky is eleven years old, two years older than Tara, but they look a lot alike. They're both tall and thin, with straight dark hair and serious dark eyes.

Tara had a floppy red hat pulled down over her hair and red plastic earrings dangling from her ears. She held up two of the duckpins. Nicky had the third one raised high in the air.

"We're not messing around," Tara said. "We're protesting."

"Protesting what?" I asked. "Cruelty to duckpins?"

Tara rolled her eyes. "Ha, ha. You're funny."

"We're protesting because you don't spend any time with us anymore," Nicky said. "You spend all your time with that new kid, Quentin."

"Give me a break," I said. "Quentin and I have to practice our act. My birthday is getting closer and closer. And we want to amaze everyone with our juggling and magic."

"But we're lonely, Max," Tara started. "And we—"

She stopped because the bedroom door swung open and my mom fluttered into the room.

Mom couldn't see Nicky and Tara. All she could see were the three pins floating in midair. Her eyes bulged nearly out of her head, and she pointed.

"Max!" Mom cried. "What's going *on*?"

2

THINK FAST, MAX. THINK FAST!

"They're . . . uh . . . duckpins," I said.

Mom stared at them floating above my head. "So?"

"Well," I said. "You know. Ducks always fly north in the spring."

She squinted at me, thinking hard about that.

Nicky and Tara let go of the duckpins and they came crashing down on my feet. "Ow!" I started hopping up and down, waiting for the pain to fade away.

"Your magic tricks are getting really good, Max," Mom said. "But most jugglers *catch* the pins."

"I know, Mom," I said, bending to rub my feet. "I'm working on it."

She left, looking confused.

Nicky and Tara popped back into view. "Your mom is funny," Tara said. "She's like a little bird twittering around the house."

"Why don't *you* go twitter around the house?" I grumbled. "I really want to practice in peace."

Nicky shook his head. He frowned at me. "You're hurting our feelings, Max."

Tara put on her pouty face. She crossed her arms in front of her. "I thought we were your best friends."

"If you two were my friends, you'd leave me alone," I snapped.

I heard a noise outside. I set the duckpins down and crossed the room to the window. I gazed out to the side of the house. A warm, sunny spring day. A small wooded lot stood next door, just trees and clumps of bushes.

And hiding behind a low evergreen bush, I saw the boy in black.

Was he a boy? Or was he an old man who looked like a boy?

I didn't know.

I only knew that this frightening guy had been following me for weeks. I tried to tell Mom and Dad about him. But they thought I was making up another ghost story.

Maybe the boy in black *was* a ghost.

He usually kept himself hidden. But one day I saw him clearly. And I saw his face change, from a boy's face to an old man's face, then back again.

I still dream about that. It's just too creepy to think about.

And there he was, lurking below, staring up at my window. Why was he following me? What did he want?

I pulled open the bedroom window and stuck my head out. I peered down at him.

He stepped out of the bushes. I couldn't see his face. It was covered in shadows from the trees. I could only see his black shirt, his black pants—and his hand, pointing up at me.

"I'm watching!" he called, in a raspy voice that sounded like dry leaves crackling. "I'm watching you!"

"Go away! Leave me alone!" I wanted to shout, but I suddenly felt too frightened. I backed away from the window and stumbled over the duckpins.

Nicky grabbed my arm and kept me from falling. "What's wrong, Max?" he asked.

"He—he's out there," I stammered. "The boy in black. I told you about him. He's always out there. Always watching me. A few weeks ago, he told me someone is going to kill me."

"Kill you?" Tara cried. "He *said* that?"

I nodded.

"He must be crazy," Nicky said. "Who would want to kill a nice guy like you?"

"Max, you're shaking!" Tara said. "You really are scared, aren't you!"

"Duh. Yeah. It's kinda scary." An idea flashed

1

into my mind. I turned to them. "You're my best friends, right?"

"Right," they both answered.

"So you'll do me a favor?"

"Sure, Max," Nicky said. "Name it. You want us to help you juggle?"

"No," I said. "I want you to go out there and find out what he wants." I glanced at the open window. "Then tell him to stop watching me. Tell him to go away."

"No problem," Nicky said.

"He can't hurt us. We're already ghosts!" Tara said.

"We'll take care of that guy," Nicky said, flashing me two thumbs up.

I watched them float right out the window.

My heart started to pound. Would they be able to get rid of him?

Or did I send my friends out to get hurt?

I moved to the window.

Keeping the front of my body pressed against the wall, I slowly leaned toward the window. I didn't want to look. But I had to. I had to know if my two ghost friends were okay.

I held my breath. I bent my head and started to peek out.

And two strong arms grabbed me roughly from behind.

3

WITH A GROAN, I twisted around—and stared into the face of my older brother, Colin. Colin, Mr. Good-Looking. Smart, Great Bod, Popular—the Golden Boy. Mr. Perfect.

Except when it comes to me. Then he's not exactly the perfect older brother. Why not? You'll see. . . .

"Hey, Blubber Butt, what's up?" he said, his perfect teeth flashing in the sunlight as he grinned at me.

"I'm kinda busy," I said, spinning back to the window. "And don't call me Blubber Butt."

"That's your real name. Blubber Butt. I saw your birth certificate."

"You don't *have* a birth certificate," I said. "You were hatched. From a dodo egg."

"Good one, Blubber Butt," he said. He slapped me on the butt—so hard that I went crashing into the wall.

"That's one thing you're getting from me on your birthday," he said.

My butt really stung. I tried to shake the pain away. "That's a birthday present?" I choked out.

He shook his blond head. "No. That's what I *won't* do on your birthday. I won't slap your butt on your birthday. As a special present."

"Gee, thanks," I said.

"And here's something else for your birthday," Colin said. He pulled back his fist, then gave me a stomach punch that made me double over and drop to my knees.

"Hee heeee heeee." I made a strange wheezing sound. I figured I'd have to walk around on all fours for the rest of my life.

"You won't be getting that on your birthday either," Colin said.

Nice guy.

He wrapped his arm around my neck and pulled me down in a headlock. Then he dug his knuckles into my head and started rubbing them back and forth until my scalp was raw.

"And as a special treat, I won't be doing that to you on your birthday," he said.

The top of my head felt soft and mushy, as if a truck had run over it. I knew I wouldn't be able to brush my hair—what was left of it—for weeks!

I was desperate to get to the window and see what was happening outside with Nicky and Tara. But Colin wouldn't let go of me. He was having a nice workout—and showing me what

I *wouldn't* be getting for my birthday at the same time.

"Colin, please—" I begged.

"For your birthday, I won't pull your nose out like this," he said. He jammed two fingers up my nostrils and stretched my nose out . . . stretched it out until I howled in pain.

Finally, Dad poked his head into my room. "Max!" he boomed. "Stop teasing Colin!"

Colin laughed and took his fingers out of my nostrils. My long, limp nose dropped down over my chin.

Colin jumped to his feet and took off after Dad. "I was just talking to Blubber Butt about his birthday presents," Colin said. "His birthday is going to be *totally* special."

"If I let him *live* that long!" Dad boomed. They both laughed, and I heard them slapping each other high fives.

Guess which one of us is Dad's favorite?

Well, I didn't have time to worry about that. I pushed my nose back into place. Then I hurried to the window to see what had happened to Nicky and Tara.

I grasped the windowsill and pushed my head out. I stared down into the wooded lot.

No one there.

I shielded my eyes from the sun with one hand and scanned the area. A fat blue jay on a low tree limb squawked at me. The trees all shimmered with fresh spring-green leaves.

But no sign of the two ghosts. Or of the boy in black.

A cold feeling swept down my body. What had happened to them?

And then, from behind me out in the hall, I heard a low moan.

A groan.

Another long moan—of pain!

Nicky and Tara!

"Help me . . . I can't walk!" I heard Tara whisper.

Another groan. And then Nicky called, "Help us! Somebody—help us!"

4

MY HEART SKIPPED A beat. What have I done? I thought. Why did I send them out there?

I stumbled to the doorway and jumped into the hall.

Nicky and Tara stood there side by side. They looked fine to me. They both were grinning.

"April Fools'," Tara said.

"You—you—you—" I sputtered. "You scared me to death! That was totally mean!"

"Maxie, you really *do* care about us!" Tara said, wrapping her arm around mine.

"Sorry, Max," Nicky said. "It was Tara's idea. She has a cold sense of humor."

Tara turned to her brother. "At least I *have* a sense of humor!"

"Please—don't start fighting," I begged.

Nicky slapped Tara on the shoulder. "Touched you last," he said.

She spun away from me, chased him down the hall, and smacked his back. "Touched you last."

She ducked away, but he touched the top of her head. "Touched you last."

"Stop it! Stop it!" I screamed.

Sometimes their "touched you last" games went on for *hours*. "Guys, please. What about the boy in black? What did he say? What did you do?"

Tara slapped Nicky's cheek. "Touched you last!" she shouted.

"The boy wasn't there," Nicky told me. He took off after Tara, who ran into my room. A few seconds later, I heard "Touched you last."

Shaking my head, I followed them inside.

"The guy had totally vanished by the time we got there," Tara said. She grabbed Nicky around the waist and tackled him to the floor. "Touched you last."

"Truce! Truce!" Nicky begged.

"I win," Tara said. She climbed off him and helped him to his feet.

Then she turned to me. "He vanished into thin air. That guy must be a ghost, Max."

Nicky's expression turned serious. "A dangerous ghost," he said softly.

"D-dangerous?" I stammered.

They both nodded. "Don't worry," Nicky said. "We'll protect you."

"Yes," Tara said, taking my arm again. "We'll stick with you, Maxie. Day and night. We'll be here when he comes back. We won't let you out of our sight."

"Uh . . . day and night?" I said.

"We'll be watching your every move," Nicky said.

I knew they were trying to be nice. But I really didn't need two ghosts at my side every minute of the day. Especially *these* two ghosts.

They were always trying to help me. But sometimes I needed help from *their* help!

"I've gotta get out of here," I said. "A little fresh air. I'll see you guys later, okay?"

They looked hurt that I didn't want them to come with me. But I needed some time to think— away from all the ghosts in my life!

I pulled my bike from the garage, jumped on it, and pedaled away. The sun felt good on my face. And the warm spring air smelled fresh and sweet.

It felt great to be pedaling hard, getting some exercise, enjoying the day without any ghosts around. Ever since Nicky and Tara had arrived, my life had been totally weird. Other ghosts and ghouls and evil creatures started popping up every time I blinked, it seemed.

Sure, I care a lot about Nicky and Tara. I'm the only one who can see and hear them. So I have to help them. But sometimes I'd like to live like a normal kid.

Whatever that means . . .

I rode to the end of my street—Bleek Street— then turned onto Powell and glided down the hill, past my school. Some kids had a softball game going on the playground. And I spotted my two *least* favorite kids from my class—the Wilbur brothers, Billy and Willy—on the basketball court. They were taking the ball away from a bunch of little kids, ruining their game and making them cry.

Typical.

I rode past the playground, swerved around a tall, skinny kid coming at me on a skateboard— and hit the brakes when I saw a girl standing at the bus stop on the corner.

Traci Wayne!

Yes! She was standing by herself, waiting for the Powell Avenue bus. The perfect time to ask her to my birthday party.

Would she say *yes,* she'd come? She had to. *Had* to!

"Hannh hannh." My tongue stuck to the roof of my mouth.

Why does that happen every time I see her?

"Hannnnh. Hannnnh."

I poked two fingers into my mouth and pulled my tongue free. Then I took a deep breath, worked up my courage, and started pedaling toward Traci.

5

I WAVED TO TRACI, but she was looking the other way, watching for the bus. As I pedaled closer, I heard a shout behind me.

I turned—and saw Nicky and Tara riding toward me on bikes. "Oh noooo," I groaned.

I put on the brakes. They rode in circles around me. "What are you doing here?" I cried. "Where did you get the bikes?"

"Borrowed them," Nicky said. "We'll return them. Really."

"We'll help you impress Traci," Tara said.

"No. Please—" I said.

"Show her how cool you are," Tara said. "Do a few X Games moves on your bike. Some awesome wheelies. She'll *beg* you to let her come to your party!"

"No. No way," I said. "I'm *begging* you two: *go away*. Don't try to help me."

"Of *course* we'll help you," Tara said. "What are friends for, Maxie?"

"Hannnnh. Hannnnnh." My tongue stuck to the roof of my mouth again. I turned and saw Traci staring at me, her eyes bulging.

She let out a scream. "Max! Those bikes—they're moving by themselves!"

Think fast, Max.

"Yes," I said. "They're dirt bikes."

Traci's mouth dropped open. "Huh?"

"They're looking for some dirt," I explained.

She squinted at me, confused.

"Let's really impress her," Tara said.

"Yeah. Let's give her something to scream about!" Nicky said.

The two ghosts were off their bikes now. Tara grabbed my handlebars. Nicky grabbed the back of the seat.

"No. Wait—" I begged. "Please—don't do this!"

"Don't do *what*?" Traci asked.

"I'm not talking to you," I said. "I'm talking to my bike."

"Here we go, Max," Tara said. "Hold on tight."

"Max, you're totally weird. Why are you talking to your bike?" Traci asked.

"Y-you'll see," I stammered.

And then the two ghosts floated into the air, carrying me and my bike with them.

I heard Traci gasp as she watched me fly off

the ground. I sailed across two parked cars, just barely making it over their roofs.

Tara flew higher, pulling up my top wheel so it looked like I was doing an awesome wheelie in midair.

Traci squealed in shock.

So did I.

"She loves it, Max. This is really impressing her," Tara said. "Hold on!"

The two ghosts spun the bike around.

"I . . . I'm getting dizzy up here," I moaned.

"Don't worry. We're bringing you down now," Nicky said.

I felt the bike start to dive. My stomach lurched into my throat. I took a deep breath, leaned forward, and gripped the handlebars tighter.

"Traci will *love* this perfect landing," Tara said.

The front of the bike dipped hard.

"Hey, Tara! Watch *out*!" I heard Nicky scream. "Watch where you're *going*!"

"Oops," Tara replied.

I felt a hard bump. It took me a second to realize my front wheel had smashed onto a car roof.

In the next second, I went flying off the bike, sailing through the air. Screaming all the way.

"Oof!" I landed hard—*on top of Traci*!

She let out a cry as we both collapsed in a heap

on the ground. I couldn't move. There I was, sprawled on her back.

She was stuck under me, her face in the dirt. "Get off! Get off me!" she sputtered.

"Uh . . . would you like to come to my birthday party?" I asked.

6

THE NEXT NIGHT, MY friend Quentin came over to rehearse our magic act. Quentin has straight blond hair and shiny blue eyes. He has dimples in both cheeks when he smiles. Girls at school think he's cute.

Tonight he wore a long-sleeved black T-shirt over baggy khaki cargo pants, torn at one knee.

I juggled three duckpins. For once, I didn't drop any. Quentin watched with a smile on his face. His eyes were so round and blue, they looked like they were made of glass.

He took the duckpins from me and pulled three red rubber balls from his magic kit. Then he juggled the duckpins *and* the red balls at the same time.

"That's excellent!" I said, touching knuckles with him and slapping a high five. I liked having Quentin over. It took my mind off the creepy guy in black.

"It's not so hard," Quentin replied, dropping

22

the balls back into his black suitcase. "I'll teach you how."

"Cool," I said. "Did you work up some new tricks for the party?"

He nodded. His smile faded. "Too bad about Traci Wayne," he said. "She really said she wouldn't come?"

"Well, I probably asked her at a bad time," I replied. "I mean, I fell on top of her, and her face was buried in dirt."

"Too bad," Quentin murmured. "If she doesn't come, none of the cool kids will come." He started pawing through his magic kit.

"Tell me something I *don't* know," I said, sighing. "Hey, I just remembered something I wanted to ask you."

He let go of the suitcase and turned to me.

"Remember a few weeks ago when my brother came in here while we were doing magic? He was giving me a hard time, and you wanted to get him out of here? So you pulled out your eyeball and held it out to him? And he totally freaked and heaved up his lunch?"

Quentin grinned at me. "An awesome moment!" he said. "You probably wonder how I did it."

"Well, yeah," I said. "It looked so real. I—"

"Watch," Quentin said. He raised his hand to his left eye, plucked it out, and held it up in the palm of his hand. The blue eye stared at me.

"Yikes!" I said. "It totally looks real."

Quentin nodded. He opened his left eye. The eyeball was still in there. He'd only pretended to pluck it out.

"This is why magicians always wear long sleeves," he said, raising his arm and tugging at the shirt cuff. "I always carry an extra eyeball with me. You never know when it will come in handy."

We both laughed.

"Now I'll show you my newest trick," he said. "We'll need a real rabbit for the night of the party. But for now I brought a stuffed rabbit."

He put the stuffed bunny rabbit into a shiny black top hat. "This trick is called the Flying Rabbit," he said. "Watch carefully, Max."

He set the top hat upside down on my computer table. Then he began to wave his hands slowly back and forth over the hat.

"Whoa, dude!" I cried out as the bunny slowly rose up from the hat.

Quentin waved his hands in the air, and the bunny floated up . . . higher . . . higher . . . The bunny rose up to the ceiling and just hung there. Then Quentin gave a fast signal with one hand—and it came shooting back down. It dropped with a *thump* back into the top hat.

"Wow," I said. "I mean, wow. That's totally awesome, Quentin."

He grinned at me. "You liked it?"

"I'm pretty good with basic hand stuff," I said. "But your tricks are like . . . *amazing*!"

His grin grew wider. He brushed his blond hair off his forehead. "It isn't that hard, really."

"Let me show you a water trick I've been practicing," I said. I started toward the bathroom to get a glass of water—but Colin stepped into the doorway and blocked my path.

"Let me out," I said. "Quentin and I are practicing for my party."

Of course my brother didn't step out of the way. Instead, he bumped me backward with his chest. Then bumped me again until I fell onto my bed.

"Hey, Blubber Butt, what's the theme of your party?" he asked, pinning me on my back.

"Theme?"

"Every cool party has a theme," Colin said. "Oh, I know. I've got the perfect one for you. How about 'armpits'?"

"I don't think so—" I started.

"Yeah. Armpits. It's perfect," Colin said. He grabbed me, dug both hands deep into my armpits, and started tickling.

"Unh unh unh!" A horrible choking sound came out of my mouth. He was tickling me so hard, I couldn't *breathe*.

"Ow! Stop! Owwww!" I pleaded and begged. But Colin kept tickling, digging his fingers in deeper and deeper.

"Owwwwww!" I shrieked in pain.

Finally, he stopped. "Maxie, you don't like that party theme?"

I glanced over at Quentin. There was something wrong with him.

He stood beside the desk, totally frozen. Not moving. Not blinking. Arms straight down. Face straight forward. Frozen still, as if he was in a trance.

I pushed Colin away and leaped off the bed. My heart pounding, I ran to my friend. "Quentin?" I cried. "Quentin? What's wrong?"

7

I GRABBED HIS SHOULDERS and shook him. "Quentin? Hey—Quentin?"

Colin came up to me and bumped me from behind. "What's up with your friend?"

"Something is wrong," I said. I shook him some more. "Quentin?"

Finally, Quentin blinked. He wrinkled his nose. He squinted at me.

I let go of his shoulders, and he staggered back a few steps.

"Quentin? What happened?" I asked.

"I . . . I'm painfully ticklish," he said finally. His hand shook as he brushed a thick strand of hair off his forehead. "It's crazy. But if I even *see* someone getting tickled, I panic."

Colin giggled. "You're joking, right?"

"It's true," Quentin insisted. "I'm so ticklish, I can't even stand to *think* about being tickled. And if I see someone else being tickled, I . . . I freeze. It's like I go into a trance state."

Colin gave me a hard shove. "Whoa, dude.

27

Your new friend is as weird as your old one, Aaron."

"Hey—cut me some slack," Quentin said. The poor guy was still trembling.

Colin raised two fingers in the air and pretended to tickle me.

"Stop it!" I shouted. "That's not funny!"

Shaking his head, Colin trotted out of the room.

I turned back to Quentin. "Are you feeling okay now?" I asked.

He nodded. "Yeah. I'm all right. But I'd better get home. It's kinda late."

I glanced at the clock. Only a little after eight. "Just let me show you my new trick," I said.

"Sorry. I'm outta here," Quentin replied. "I'm working on a project at home and I want to get back to it. You know, I build things too."

"Cool," I said. I walked him downstairs to the front door. "Sorry about Colin," I said. "He's kind of a jerk."

"Kind of," Quentin murmured.

We both laughed. My armpits still burned as if they were on fire.

I said good night to Quentin and climbed back upstairs. I could hear the TV on in Colin's room at the end of the hall. When I walked into my room, Nicky and Tara were waiting for me.

"There's something strange about Quentin,"

Tara said. She was pacing back and forth, pulling at her long earrings. She does that when she's stressed or when she's thinking hard about something.

"Don't pick on Quentin," I said. "He had a rough night."

"That's just my point," Tara replied. She stopped pacing and stared at me. "There's something totally weird about how he just froze like that. Like he's a robot and his circuits blew out."

"You've been seeing too many dumb movies," I said. "He explained what happened. He's just very ticklish."

"Hel-*lo*. No one is *that* ticklish," Nicky said. He was sitting on my bed, juggling one duckpin between his hands. "No one goes into a trance because someone *else* is being tickled."

"Quentin does," I said, frowning at him. "Since when are you a tickling expert?"

"There's something else very strange about him," Tara said. One of her earrings had gotten tangled in her floppy hat, and she struggled to free it.

I rolled my eyes. "What else?"

"His magic is too good," she replied. "Way too good."

"I hate to say it, but Tara is right," Nicky said, tossing up the duckpin. "There's something very suspicious about Quentin."

I let out a long sigh. "You two are just jealous," I snapped. "You're jealous because he's my best friend now."

Tara laughed. "Us? Jealous? You're joking, right?"

"Hel-*lo*," Nicky said. "We're just looking out for you, Max. You've already got that weird boy in black following you."

"Whoa. Wait!" Tara stopped pacing and clapped her hands together. "That's it! Quentin is working with that weird ghost in black. They're pals, and they're working together."

Nicky nodded. "One outside the house and one inside," he said.

"Stop it. You're both crazy!" I cried. "Quentin is my friend. He isn't a robot or a ghost. He's a kid who's very ticklish and very good at magic. That's all."

"He's up to no good," Nicky said. He dropped the duckpin and jumped to his feet. "I know he is. Tara and I are going to prove it."

"Leave him alone," I shouted. "I mean it. He's my friend, and he's a good guy."

"We'll see . . . ," Tara said.

I started to reply, but Colin's voice boomed from his room down the hall. "Max, get in here! Hurry!"

Uh-oh. Now what?

8

COLIN WAS LYING ON his bed with a big bag of potato chips cradled under one arm. When I walked up close to him, he spit a mouthful of chips at me, then laughed.

"Is that why you called me in?" I asked, wiping the glop off my face.

He jammed another handful of chips into his mouth. When I reached for the bag, he swiped it away from me.

"Give me a break. What do you want?" I asked.

He chewed loudly and pointed to the TV. It looked like some kind of news show.

"What are you watching?" I asked.

"It's *The Best News Bloopers of the Year* on Channel 600," he said. "Watch what's next."

Channel 600 is our local TV station, and I knew what was coming up next. A heavy feeling of dread swept down over me as I watched the next news blooper.

Because there I was. Last month, at the dedication of the new swimming pool at my school. I was chosen to give the school trophy to Mayor Stank. It was supposed to be a big day for me, but it got messed up.

It got messed up because of Nicky and Tara. They showed up and tried to help me, as usual. They tried to help me give the trophy to the mayor.

Instead, things got a little out of control. I clonked the mayor in the head with the trophy by accident, and he fell into the pool.

That's bad luck, right? Want to hear *more* bad luck?

Mayor Stank didn't know how to swim.

So he was spluttering and sputtering and screaming his head off, bobbing around helplessly in the water.

The teachers were all frozen in shock. So I reached in to try to rescue him—and accidentally pulled his pants off.

Ha, ha. Funny blooper, huh?

No one has let me forget it. Colin teases me about it every day. Billy and Willy, the Wilbur brothers, acted the whole scene out at the talent show at school last week.

And now there I was on Channel 600, knocking Mayor Stank into the water again. And again. And again. One of the best news bloopers of the year.

"Hey, thanks for sharing that," I told my brother.

He laughed. "Face it, Maxie. Your whole life is a blooper."

I started toward the door. "Just leave me alone, okay?" I snapped. "I'm not in a good mood."

Colin's smile faded. He sat up. "Hey, come back," he said. "Here." He tossed me the bag of potato chips.

I caught it in both hands. "Thanks," I said. I pulled out a few chips and shoved them into my mouth. "Did you spit on them?"

"No way," he said. He slapped the bed. "Come here. Sit down."

"You've injured me enough today," I said, backing away. "I'm going to have to sleep with ice cubes in my armpits."

"I'm not going to hurt you," he said, raising his right hand to swear. "Sit down. Let's have a talk. Why are you in a bad mood?"

I stopped with a handful of potato chips halfway to my mouth. "You're kidding, right? You want to have a talk with *me*?"

The last time Colin and I had a "talk," I was black and blue for a month.

"Sit down, Max," he said. "I'm your big brother. Maybe I can help."

He looked totally serious. I inched my way back over to him. I tensed up, waiting for him to jump me and punch my lights out. Or maybe dump the potato chip bag down the back of my shirt.

But no. He sat there on the edge of the bed with his hands at his sides. "What's up with you, bro?" he asked. "Tell me what's wrong."

I sat down next to him. "No way can I tell you," I said. "If I tell you something, you'll just go running to Mom and Dad to tell them I'm still making up crazy ghost stories. You know what Dad said. He said he'd ground me for life if I don't give up the ghost stories."

"I know," Colin replied. He didn't laugh at me. His expression was serious. Thoughtful.

"I won't tell on you, Max," he said softly. "I just want to be a big brother to you." He gave me a gentle shove. "Hey, you're turning twelve. It's time for you and me to be buddies."

Was I dreaming this?

"Okay," I said. "I'll tell you why I'm in a bad mood."

I took a deep breath, then told him about the boy in black. "He's been watching me for weeks," I said. "He follows me everywhere I go. And I've seen his face change. From young to old, then back again. I'm really scared. He must be some kind of ghost, don't you think?"

Colin stared at me for a long moment. A smile slowly spread over his face.

He jumped up, using my shoulder to hoist himself to his feet. Then he ran out into the hall. And I heard him running downstairs, yelling at the top of his voice:

"Mom! Dad! You won't believe this! Max is still making up ghost stories!"

9

ON MY WAY TO school Monday morning, I saw the boy in black.

As I walked he stayed half a block behind me, ducking behind bushes and hedges.

I stopped and turned around, my backpack swinging. I saw him dive behind a tree.

A shiver ran down my body.

He was like my shadow. A dark, evil shadow.

What did he want? Why was he watching me?

I kept hearing his warning to me, the words he'd rasped in my ear:

"Don't you understand? They're going to kill *you. They're going to* kill *you!"*

Who did he mean? Who wanted to kill me?

Was he going to hurt me?

My heart pounded in my chest.

I just wanted him to vanish, disappear forever. I wanted to turn around and not see that dark shadow with those silvery eyes locked on me.

But I could see him peeking out at me from behind the wide tree trunk, waiting for me to move on so he could move on too.

And I spun around and took off, running the rest of the way to school. My backpack bounced hard on my back. I thought about Nicky and Tara and what they'd said about Quentin.

"There's something very suspicious about Quentin."

"Quentin is working with that weird ghost in black. They're pals, and they're working together."

To do *what*?

The whole idea was crazy. I refused to believe any of it.

Nicky and Tara had been wrong before. And they were wrong now. They were wrong about Quentin.

I ran up the front steps of my school and glanced back just before I stepped through the double doors. The boy in black stood across the street—in plain view. He stood between two cars, watching me . . . just watching.

I shivered again, glad to have the doors close behind me. I felt safe in school. But what would be waiting for me when I stepped back outside?

That afternoon, I went to return a bottle of glue to the art supply closet, and I spotted Traci Wayne in the pottery room.

I peeked through the doorway. I saw the low gray kiln against the back wall. The other walls had tall shelves for holding all the pots and bowls and things kids made. Two long worktables stood beside rows of pottery wheels.

Traci sat at one of the wheels, working with clay. She didn't see me. She was concentrating on her work, her head down as she molded wet red clay, forming a bowl on the spinning wheel.

"Hannnnh hunnnnh." My tongue stuck to the roof of my mouth, as usual. My heart started to do a hip-hop rhythm in my chest.

I glanced around. Traci was all alone in the pottery room. This was a perfect time to try once again to invite her to my birthday party.

"Hannnhh. Thannnnth." I pulled my tongue free and stepped into the room. My legs were shaking, so I sat down at a pottery wheel across from her.

"Hi, Traci," I managed to say.

Her hands were smoothing a bowl as it spun. She glanced up from her work. "Oh no," she groaned. "Please don't fall on me, Max."

"I can't fall on you," I said. "I'm sitting down."

"Oh, thank goodness," she said, sighing.

I took a deep breath. "Traci, I just wanted to ask you—" I started. But I stopped when my wheel started spinning.

Hey—I didn't turn it on. What's up with this? I wondered.

And then I saw a big glob of clay come flying across the room and land on my wheel as it started to pick up speed.

The red clay plopped onto the pottery wheel in front of me. And then I felt someone grab my hands and push them onto the clay.

And I knew.

I knew Nicky and Tara were back. Invisible. Trying to help me again.

"Max, I didn't know you were into pottery," Traci said, without looking up from her work.

"Oh, yes," I replied. "I love it. I pot all the time. Every chance I get, I just sit down and start potting."

Another big glob of wet clay landed on my wheel. I tried to smooth it down, but some of it shot off. The wheel was spinning too fast.

"Traci, can I ask you a question?" I said.

The wheel picked up speed. I pushed my hands into the wet clay and tried to mold it into a nice bowl shape. But another glob of clay flew down and hit the wheel.

"Stop it! Stop it!" I whispered to Nicky and Tara.

Traci glanced up. "I can't stop now. The clay will dry and harden. Why do you want me to stop?"

"I wasn't talking to you," I said. "I was talking to the wheel. I always talk to the wheel."

"Were you *born* weird?" Traci asked.

I didn't really know how to answer that.

Plop! More clay dropped onto the wheel. Gobs of clay flew off in all directions.

"Hey!" Traci let out a startled cry as a flying red clay blob smacked into her forehead. "Watch it, Max!"

Too late.

A huge hunk of clay spun off my wheel, flew into the air, and landed in Traci's hair. She let out a scream. Her hands shot up to her head, and her bowl fell off the wheel and plopped onto the floor.

Big pieces of clay flew off my wheel and splattered the wall and ceiling. "Stop it!" I screamed to Nicky and Tara. "Can't you stop this—*gulp!*"

A glob of wet clay flew into my open mouth. I started to choke.

Traci jumped to her feet. "I'm *outta* here!" she cried. She took two steps, slipped in a puddle of clay, and fell on her face.

I swallowed the clay in my mouth. It didn't taste too bad. I glanced down at Traci. She was covered from head to foot in the wet, sticky stuff.

I reached down to help her up. But my hand

was smeared with slippery clay, and she slipped and fell right back down.

Finally, I tugged her up with both hands.

My big chance, I thought.

"Traci," I said, "will you come to my birthday party?"

10

TRACI STAGGERED BACK, rubbing smears of clay off her face. "Okay, yes," she said.

"Hannnh thannnnnth." I started to swallow my tongue, but I pulled it out in time.

I blinked ten or twelve times. "What did you say?" I asked finally.

She pulled a clot of clay from her blond hair. A big chunk of hair came with it. "I said yes," she repeated. "Yes, I'll come to your party, Max—*if* you promise never to come near me again. Ever."

"You really will come?" I cried. My voice came out so high and shrill, I sounded like SpongeBob SquarePants.

She nodded. "If you promise to stay away from me forever," she said.

"That's fair," I replied, rubbing clay off my front teeth. "That's totally fair. Awesome!"

Pulling clay off her T-shirt, Traci staggered from the room.

I gazed after her for a while. Then I spun

around angrily. "Nicky? Tara? Where are you?" I shouted. "How could you do that to me?"

"Do what?" Tara asked. She came into view standing beside a potter's wheel, tossing a ball of clay from hand to hand. Nicky popped into view sitting at the next wheel, sculpting a long, slender vase.

"Look at this mess!" I cried, waving my arms around. "Look at me. I'm covered in clay! It's all your fault!"

"And it's all our fault that Traci is coming to your party," Tara replied.

"We helped you, Max. Admit it," Nicky said.

That's when I lost it.

"I'll tell you what you did. You made a horrible mess!" I shouted. "I want you to leave me alone. Do you hear me? Leave me alone!"

And at that moment, Ms. Delaney, the art teacher, stepped into the room. "Max? Who are you talking to? You're all alone in here. Why are you shouting that you want to be left alone?"

"Uh . . . I'm practicing," I said. "In case someone comes in."

Behind her round black glasses, her eyes squinted hard. She was staring at Nicky's vase, going round and round on the wheel.

"M-Max—" she stammered. "That vase. It's spinning on the wheel with no one there."

"I know," I said. "It's a do-it-yourself project."

"Good one, Max," Nicky said, grinning at me from behind the wheel.

"Go away," I said. "I mean it."

Ms. Delaney gasped. "What did you say?"

"I said, 'How are you today?'" I told her.

Then her mouth fell open and she dropped the stack of construction paper she'd been holding. "Oh, my goodness! Max! Look at this room! What have you done?"

"Uh . . . I'm redecorating," I said. "Giving it sort of a primitive *hut* look."

She shook her head. "Clay everywhere," she muttered. "We'll never get this cleaned up. Never."

"Tell her you think it's an improvement," Tara said.

"Just shut up!" I said.

Ms. Delaney gasped. "Max, have you lost your mind? Since when do you tell a teacher to shut up?"

"Do you see the trouble you get me into?" I shouted at the two ghosts.

"*Me?*" Ms. Delaney gasped. "How did I get you into trouble? I think your own *big mouth* got you into trouble!"

"Ha, ha. Score one for her!" Nicky said.

"I'll shut you up later," I told him.

"I don't think so," Ms. Delaney said. She grabbed my arm and started dragging me to the

44

door. "I have no choice, Max. I'm taking you to the principal's office. Maybe Mrs. Wright can find out what your problem is."

"*You're* my problem!" I cried, shaking my fist at Nicky and Tara. "This is the *last straw*! You're not invited to my birthday party. I mean it—stay away! You can't come to my party!"

Ms. Delaney squinted at me. "Party? What party? Why would I come to your party?"

"I'm not talking to you," I said.

Mrs. Wright greeted us at the door to her office. "Max? You're back again?" she said. "Come in. Take your usual seat, and we'll have a nice long talk."

11

AT DINNER THAT NIGHT, Mom was very upset. She told Dad the whole story. "The principal called me this afternoon. Max told a teacher to shut up. And he tossed clay all over the art room."

Dad's face turned even redder than usual. Steam started to pour from his ears. He gripped his fork and knife in his big, meaty fists. "In trouble again? Why did you do that, Max?"

"Hard to explain," I muttered.

The dragon tattoo on Dad's right bicep appeared to lower its fiery head and stare at me. "Why can't you be more like Colin?" Dad growled. "Is that asking too much? Colin is perfect. Why can't you be perfect?"

"I don't know," I whispered, head down.

Colin kicked me hard under the table. Then, grinning, he pulled out a sheet of paper. "Here is my new honor roll certificate," he told Dad. "Would you like to get it framed like all the others?"

I was grounded for a week. I didn't see Nicky

or Tara the whole time. I knew they were angry at me. Angry because I'd told them to stay away from my birthday party.

But I didn't expect them to totally disappear.

A week after the pottery room incident, Quentin came over to practice magic tricks. My party was only a few days away. I wanted to rehearse and rehearse until our act was perfect.

After all, Traci Wayne was coming. I wasn't allowed to get near her. But this was my big chance to impress her.

"Let me show you a hat trick that everyone loves," Quentin said. "Do you have a real hat I could use?"

I rubbed my chin, thinking hard. "No. I only have baseball caps," I said. "Oh, wait. My dad has a really good hat he uses for weddings and funerals and things."

"Go get it," Quentin said. "You'll like this trick."

I hesitated. "But it's my dad's only hat, and it's very expensive. You have to be very careful."

"No problem," Quentin said. "The trick is perfectly safe. I've done it a thousand times."

I went down to my parents' bedroom closet to borrow Dad's hat. He and Mom were in the den, watching wrestling on TV. They were both shouting at the screen: "Kill him! Kill! Kill! Break him in two!"

47

They both love wrestling. But sometimes they get carried away. Last week after a big match, Mom jumped on Dad and started slapping his bald head with both hands. He had to pick her up and carry her into the shower to snap her out of it.

I pulled Dad's hat down from the top shelf. And I also borrowed one of his neckties. He only has three, but I don't think I've ever seen him wear one. I had learned a nifty new necktie trick that I knew Quentin would love.

"Kill! Kill! Ruin him!" My parents' shouts rang out from the den.

Back in my room, I handed Quentin the hat. "What's the trick?" I asked. "Will it be good for the party?"

He nodded. He pulled a few things from his magic kit. He held up two eggs. "I crack these two eggs into the hat," he said. "Then I pour in this jar of honey. Then I turn the hat right side up, and it's perfectly dry."

I gulped. "Are you sure about this?"

"Of course I'm sure," Quentin said. "It's an easy trick. Watch."

He pushed his blond hair off his forehead. Then he cracked the two eggs and let them run into the hat. Then he opened the honey jar and turned it upside down, and the honey slowly oozed into the hat with the egg yolks.

"Say the magic words!" Quentin cried. "Hat be good!" He turned the hat over—and honey and yellow egg yolk came dripping out.

"You—you ruined my dad's hat!" I wailed.

Quentin squinted at the sticky mess inside the hat. "I don't get it. That trick always works."

My heart started leaping in my chest. I shoved the hat under my bed. Later I'd have to figure out a good hiding place for it.

"What's up with the necktie?" Quentin asked, picking up the tie and pulling it through his fingers.

"Here's a good trick for the party," I said. "And this one is totally safe."

I took the tie from him and picked up a pair of scissors. "See? I make it look like I cut the tie into four pieces. But I don't really cut it. I cut this piece of cloth instead."

I pulled the cloth from my magic kit and tucked it under the tie. "Now watch," I said. "It looks like I've cut the tie up. But when I tug on it, it's all together again."

"Cool," Quentin muttered.

"Ladies and gentlemen," I boomed, holding the tie in front of me. "The Amazing Indestructible Necktie!"

I snipped it into four pieces. I balled the pieces up in my hand. And then I gave a hard tug. "Back together again!" I exclaimed.

Wrong.

I'd sliced my dad's tie into four pieces.

"Oh, wow." I stared at the pieces of tie in my hand.

Then I pictured my dad, as big as a truck, a bellowing bull when he was angry. When he saw what I'd done to his hat and tie, he'd . . . he'd . . .

I couldn't even think about it.

Trembling, I shoved the pieces of necktie under my bed next to the hat.

Quentin tried a few easy card tricks. The cards fell from his hands and scattered over the floor. He tried the trick where he waves his magic wand and it turns into a bouquet of flowers. It didn't work. The wand broke in two.

He shook his head. "Max, everything is messed up tonight. I can't figure out why."

I could.

I knew what was happening. Nicky and Tara were messing up our tricks.

I gritted my teeth and balled my hands into fists. I felt so angry, I wanted to scream.

But *no way* could I tell Quentin about them.

Nicky and Tara were angry because they couldn't come to my party. So they were doing their best to mess up our magic act.

We tried a few more easy tricks, and they were ruined too. "It just isn't our night," Quentin said. "Maybe we should try again tomorrow night."

He left, shaking his head, very confused.

As soon as he was out the door, my two ghost friends appeared. "How's it going, Max?" Tara asked, grinning at me.

"You *know* how it's going," I snapped.

"Did you have a bad night?" Nicky asked, acting innocent.

I realized I was grinding my teeth. I'd never been so angry at them. "You have no right to do that," I shouted. "You have no right to ruin all our tricks."

"I'll bet your tricks will go a lot better if you invite us to your party," Tara said.

"For sure," Nicky chimed in. "Invite us to your birthday party, and we'll be your best friends again."

"No way!" I cried. "You're not my best friends. And stop begging me. No way are you coming to my party!"

They both put on these really hurt faces. Tara pulled off her hat, tossed it on the floor, and started stomping on it.

I turned away from them and walked to the window. I took deep breaths, trying to calm down. I didn't like being angry at them. They were two poor young ghosts, after all. They probably wouldn't have any more birthdays—because they were dead.

But messing up our magic tricks like that was just plain mean.

I gazed out the window, pressing my forehead against the cool glass. A few stars twinkled dimly in the night sky. I lowered my eyes—and gasped when I saw the boy in black staring up at me.

He stood at the side of my yard, leaning against a tree trunk.

I pulled up the window, stuck my head out, and shouted down at him. "Go away! I'm warning you! Go away!"

He took a few steps closer to the house. Light from the kitchen downstairs washed over him, and I saw his face. An old man's face, lined and wrinkled and sagging.

He cupped his hands around his mouth and called up to me. "Be careful!"

Gripping the windowsill, I stared down at his ancient face, at his pale, sunken eyes. "What do you want?" I screamed. "Why are you doing this?"

"Be careful," he repeated in a breathy rasp of a voice. "They are going to kill you. The ghosts are going to kill you!"

A chill ran down my back. I stepped away from the window. Shivering, I turned to Nicky and Tara.

"What did he mean?" I asked. "Why did he say that? Why did he say you are going to *kill* me?"

I saw the shock on Nicky's and Tara's faces. And then they disappeared.

12

I SAT DOWN AND tried to do some math homework for about an hour. Math is one of my favorite subjects. The problems were easy, but after seeing the boy in black, it was hard to concentrate. Working on the math eventually helped me to push him from my thoughts, so I ended up doing the next day's assignment too.

The kids at school call me Brainimon. That's because I have a good brain and I get all A's.

Mom thinks I'm really popular, because she hears my phone ring at least four or five times a night. But it's only kids asking me for help with their homework.

When I finished my homework, I tried to IM my friend Aaron. But he wasn't online.

That's when I saw the little metal suitcase against the wall. Quentin's magic kit. He had forgotten it.

I picked it up by the handle, then sat down with it on my lap. I was tempted to open it and see what he had inside.

But I decided that wouldn't be right. No magician likes to share his secrets.

Quentin had his name and address on a tag tied to the handle of the case. I read it and saw that he lived on Murk Drive. That's in a pretty fancy neighborhood about four or five blocks from my house. Lots of big houses and mansions hidden behind tall hedges.

I glanced at the clock. Only eight-thirty. Mom and Dad wouldn't mind if I walked over to Quentin's house and returned the case to him.

I brushed my hair, changed my T-shirt, picked up the heavy case, and started to the door.

"Whoa. Where are you going, Max?" Nicky and Tara blocked my path.

"Out," I said.

They both gazed at the metal suitcase. "You're taking that to Quentin's?" Tara asked.

I nodded. "Yes, if you'll get out of my way."

"Are you sure you want to go there alone?" Nicky asked.

"There's something very suspicious about Quentin," Tara said.

"Maybe there's something suspicious about you!" I said. "Why did the boy in black say you were going to *kill* me?"

"We don't know, Max," Nicky said.

"We really don't," Tara agreed. "You don't

have to worry about us. It's that weirdo Quentin you should worry about!"

I rolled my eyes. "Give me a break," I muttered. "And stop saying that. There's nothing weird or suspicious about Quentin. Now, can I get out my own door?"

"Okay, okay," Nicky said, moving aside.

"What a grouch," Tara said. "We're only thinking of you, Max."

"Yeah. Sure," I said, stepping into the hall and heading to the stairs.

Tara put her hand on my shoulder. "Be careful, okay, Max? Be very careful."

I shut the front door behind me and stepped out into the warm, windy night. The trees were shaking their new leaves. The freshly cut grass gleamed under a bright full moon.

I made my way toward Murk Drive, thinking about Nicky and Tara. They were angry about the birthday party. That was why they tried to scare me about going to Quentin's house.

There's nothing to worry about, I told myself. What's the big deal?

13

A FEW MINUTES LATER, I turned the corner onto Murk Drive. I could see the tops of the big stone and brick houses with their tall chimneys and slanted roofs. Tall hedges—way above my head—lined both sides of the street.

The streetlamps looked old-fashioned. They cast an eerie silvery light over the sidewalks and hedges. As I walked along, the gusting wind shook the hedges and made them whisper.

I followed the numbers on the mailboxes and stopped in front of Quentin's house. At first, I couldn't see the house because the hedge was too tall.

I moved to the cobblestone driveway and gazed up the long front yard to the house. A tall brick house with chimneys on both sides, shutters on all the windows, and a wide front porch.

The front of the house was dark. But I could see light pouring from some of the side windows. The long driveway curled around to the back, where I glimpsed a wide garage.

Wow, Quentin lives in a *mansion*! I thought.

I suddenly wondered if he had any brothers and sisters to share this huge house with. He had never mentioned any. In fact, he had never even talked about his mom or dad.

I took a few steps toward the house—and the tall hedge trembled as if coming alive!

I jumped back.

"Whoa." I scolded myself for getting scared of a hedge.

Quentin's magic kit suddenly felt very heavy. I switched hands and started to walk up the long driveway. A bed of tulips lined each side of the drive. And I saw other flower gardens near the front of the house.

I climbed the stone steps onto the front porch and walked up to the broad front door. I set the case down and listened. I couldn't hear any-one inside.

I knocked on the door. Then I knocked harder. My fist didn't make much of a sound on the solid wood.

No sound from inside.

I spotted a brass doorbell to the right of the door. I pressed the button once, twice, then held it down for a while.

I couldn't hear it ringing inside. Was it broken?

I raised my hand to knock again—but decided to try the doorknob instead.

I turned it and pushed. The door creaked loudly as I opened it just enough to poke my head in. "Anyone home?" I called.

My voice echoed down a long hallway.

"Quentin? It's me, Max!" I shouted.

Silence. From somewhere inside I could hear the loud ticking of a clock.

"Quentin?"

He had to be in there. He'd told me he was going straight home. He just couldn't hear me in this enormous mansion.

I hoisted up the magic kit and dragged it into the house.

"Hey, Quentin? It's me!" I tried again. My voice echoed down the long halls. It reminded me of the caves in Kentucky my family had visited when Colin and I were little. You could shout your name and hear it repeated six times.

My eyes slowly adjusted to the darkness. I could see that I was in a long entryway. I took a few steps into the house. The entryway led past a huge living room. I could see big couches and enormous paintings on the wall.

"Hey! Quentin?"

I stopped and listened for a reply. Silence.

I followed the hall past the living room. My shoes didn't make a sound as they sank into the thick carpet.

I heard a creaking sound behind me and

realized it was the front door blowing back and forth in the wind.

"Hel-*lo*! Anyone here?"

Yellow light poured out from an open door at the end of the hall. I walked past a snarling tiger's head mounted high over a closed door.

Dragging the metal suitcase, I stepped past a display of old pistols in a glass case. The pistols were shiny and polished and looked like they'd appeared in old movies.

Quentin never mentioned that his dad collects old guns, I thought. Then I remembered once again that Quentin had never mentioned his dad at all.

Did Quentin's dad shoot that tiger? I wondered.

I stepped into the square of yellow light on the carpet. Somewhere to my right I heard a loud hum, like the sound of a refrigerator starting up.

Silence everywhere else.

I cleared my throat and tried once again. "Quentin? It's me. Max."

I stepped into the lighted room. I saw bookshelves that ran up to the ceilings. Another animal head on the wall, this one a deer. Under it, a fireplace, dark and empty.

I turned and saw the back of a wide armchair, a hand draped over the side.

"Hello?" I called. "Quentin?"

I set down the case and walked closer. Someone was sitting in the chair but didn't move when I called. Was he asleep?

"Hello?"

I stepped up to the side of the chair. And stared at Quentin.

It was Quentin's body. I recognized his shirt. His jeans.

Yes. Quentin's body slouched in the chair. *With no head.*

No head on his shoulders.

Quentin sitting there, *headless*!

And then I saw his head resting in his lap. Faceup. His head staring up from his lap.

And I opened my mouth to scream.

14

I OPENED MY MOUTH to scream—but no sound came out. My breath caught in my throat.

I gasped when I heard footsteps.

Soft thuds in the carpeted hall. Coming my way.

Who was it?

A wave of nausea tightened my stomach. I swallowed hard, trying to keep my dinner down.

The soft, thudding footsteps moved slowly, steadily.

I glanced around the room. Nowhere to hide.

I heard a cough at the doorway.

I spun around—and stared at Quentin!

"Max, hi," he said. "Did you ring the front bell? I didn't hear it."

"Wh-wh-wh—" I sputtered. I couldn't force any words out. My whole body was shaking.

Quentin didn't seem to notice. He walked over to the chair. "I was down in the basement," he said. "I was getting parts for Quentin Junior here."

"I—I thought—" I started.

He picked up the Quentin head and raised it to the neck of the body. Now I could see that it was like a dummy. Like a ventriloquist's dummy.

Quentin held the head up, then cradled it in one arm. "What do you think? It's awesome, right?"

"Awesome," I said, still shaking.

"I told you I was working on a cool project," Quentin said. "If I get this dummy finished, I'm going to build one for you. You know. For your birthday present."

"Th-thanks," I stammered.

Quentin stared at me. He laughed. "Hel-*lo*. You didn't really think this was me, did you?"

"Uh . . . no way," I lied. "Of course not. I . . . I'm just shaking like this because it's cold in here."

I held up his suitcase. "You left your magic kit at my house," I said, starting to feel normal again. "So I brought it over."

"Hey, thanks, Max." He put down the dummy and took the case from me. "Want to come see my theater? My dad built me a stage and everything for performing magic."

"I'd better get home," I said. "I didn't tell my parents I was going out."

He walked me down the long hall to the door. "Thanks for bringing my case. See you at school," he said.

As I walked home, I got angrier and angrier.

I never would have scared myself over that dummy if Nicky and Tara hadn't put bad thoughts in my head.

The two ghosts had said Quentin was suspicious. Nicky said he was a robot. Tara said his magic was too good. That there was something weird about him.

They'd put all those bad ideas in my head.

So it was *no wonder* I got scared when I saw that headless dummy in the chair.

Nicky and Tara were waiting when I stormed into my room a few minutes later. "How did it go, Max?" Tara asked.

"Fine," I said. "Quentin is a totally normal guy. And he's a good friend. And I don't want you *ever* to say another bad word about him."

"Okay, okay," Tara said, raising both hands as if in surrender. "Excuse me for living!"

"You're *not* living!" I snapped. "You're a ghost. You both are. And you have no right to mess up my life!"

Their mouths dropped open and they looked shocked.

"Fine. Just fine," Tara said. "Nicky and I can take a hint. Don't worry, Max. Don't look for us at your party."

Nicky crossed his arms in front of him.

64

"We wouldn't be caught *dead* at your party!" he said.

"Happy birthday anyway, Max," Tara said. "Have a great party—without us. Good luck."

"You'll need it," Nicky said.

What did he mean by that?

15

TENSE.

That's how I'd describe the start of my birthday party.

Kids from my class started arriving around four o'clock. I kept checking my watch and looking for Traci. No sign of her.

By four-thirty, Marci Gold, Ashley Fromm, and a lot of Traci's other friends had arrived. But there was no sign of Traci.

My dad went bowling with some of his buddies, so I didn't have to worry about him. And that morning, I'd begged my mom to stay out of sight.

I tried to explain to her that if you're twelve years old, it's just not cool to have your mom all over your party, acting like you're six.

She didn't seem to like that.

And she totally didn't listen.

She stood at the front door greeting everyone as if it was *her* party. She stopped every kid and said how grown-up they looked and how tall they'd gotten.

Yikes.

She kept fluttering around the living room and den, *talking* to my friends. It was *so* not cool.

And then she came over to me and said, "Maxie, dear, isn't the music too loud? Everyone has to shout."

"Mom, it's a *party*!" I screamed.

A lot of kids heard me and laughed.

The cool kids all hung together in the hall and didn't mix with any of the other kids. I kept checking my watch every two minutes. Where was Traci?

The phone rang. I ran to answer it. It was my friend Aaron's mother. She said Aaron couldn't come to my party because he was grounded.

He had torn all the stuffing out of his little sister's teddy bear and turned it into a hand puppet. I could hear his sister, Kaytlin, sobbing and sobbing in the background.

Aaron was always doing stuff like that. I'm sure he'd just wanted to give his sister a nice surprise. But it didn't work out.

Aaron and I were really good buddies. But I didn't see him much these days. We mostly IM'd each other—because he was grounded just about every day of his life.

"Well, that's bad news," I told my mom.

"At least Quentin is here," Mom said.

Quentin was upstairs in my room, practicing

the magic tricks we were going to perform in a few minutes.

I checked my watch. Nearly five o'clock. Where was Traci?

"I have to leave for a few minutes," Mom called from across the room. "I have to go to the bakery and pick up your cake."

And then she shouted really loudly, "You won't play any kissing games while I'm gone, will you?"

Gulp.

I started to choke.

Everyone heard her. Everyone.

How embarrassing is that?

I wanted to hide. Marci and Ashley were laughing at me. And the other cool kids were all rolling their eyes and snickering and sneering.

Of course, things got worse.

As soon as Mom was out the door, Billy and Willy, the Wilbur brothers, started showing off, wrestling on the living room floor.

Kids started cheering and clapping. Until the Wilburs heaved into the coffee table and knocked over the tall glass lamp.

I let out a cry.

My mom's favorite lamp!

It smashed to the floor and shattered into a million pieces. Glass flew everywhere.

Kids were screaming and laughing. Someone

stepped on a chunk of glass and it made a loud crunch.

I stormed over to Billy and Willy. "What is your *problem*?" I shouted.

"We didn't do it," Willy said. "It just fell."

"He's right," Billy said. "We didn't touch it."

"We'll clean it up," Willy said. "Where's the broom? In the garage?"

He and his brother ran to the kitchen.

"No!" I cried. "Don't open the back door! Don't open the back door!"

Too late.

They opened the back door—and Buster, our dog, came stampeding in.

Buster is huge. He's a wolfhound. He looks like a really hairy panther! And for some reason, he *hates* me!

That's one reason we don't let him in the house.

"Stop him! Stop him!" I shouted to the Wilbur brothers.

Too late.

The big monster came racing in, all excited, his furry tail beating back and forth. He stuck his snout into a bowl of pretzels and gobbled them up without even chewing.

"Go, Buster! Go, Buster!" The Wilburs started clapping their hands and chanting.

Buster turned and gazed at the crowd. Then

his eyes settled on me. Instantly, he lowered his head and started to growl.

"Good boy," I said. "Good Buster. Let's go back outside, okay?"

He snarled in reply and bared his teeth.

Kids backed out of the way. A few kids screamed.

"Go, Buster! Go, Buster!" The Wilburs continued their chant.

"Good boy, Buster," I said, trying to keep calm in front of everyone. "It's my birthday, Buster. You wouldn't damage me on my birthday—would you?"

The big monster let out another growl and leaped for my throat.

I ducked and he went sailing over me.

"Go, Buster! Go, Buster!" the Wilburs sang.

Why had Mom made me invite those two jerks?

Buster landed on all fours. He spun around quickly. Dove forward. And wrapped his teeth around my ankle.

"Owwww!" I let out a furious cry. "Not on my birthday! Not on my birthday!"

I was on my back on the floor now. Twisting and squirming in pain. Shouting. Struggling to pull my ankle from the dog's jaws.

"Go, Buster! Go, Buster!"

That's when the front door opened and Mom

walked in, carrying the cake box in both hands. She stopped in the living room doorway and squinted at me.

"Max? Are you playing with the dog and forgetting about your guests?"

16

MOM PULLED THE DOG off my ankle by bribing him with a dog biscuit. He followed her peacefully out to the backyard.

I limped over to Marci and Ashley and the other cool kids, who were still hanging out by themselves in the hall. My ankle throbbed with pain, and it was starting to swell.

"Where is Traci?" I asked her friends. "She should have been here an hour ago."

Marci and Ashley shrugged. "We haven't heard from her."

"I know," I said. "I'll call her cell and find out what's taking her so long."

"Good idea," Marci said.

"Do you have her cell number?" I asked.

"She wouldn't want you to have her cell number," Marci said.

"Oh. Right," I said.

I didn't have any more time to think about Traci. I heard someone stomping noisily down the stairs. I turned in time to see Colin pushing his way through my friends.

He'd promised me he'd stay up in his room and not try to ruin my party.

But he'd never kept a promise in his life. Why should today be different?

"Where is Blubber Butt?" he asked the cool kids in the hall. "Have you seen Blubber Butt?"

He turned and saw me. "Hey! There you are. Guess what I'm *not* going to call you on your birthday?"

"Why don't you call me long distance?" I muttered.

Colin laughed. "Good one, Blubber Butt."

Mom was at the dining room table, putting candles on my birthday cake. "Colin," she said. "Don't call your brother names on his birthday."

"I'm not," Colin told her. He turned to me with a grin. "Happy birthday, little bro." And he slapped me on the back, so hard I heard cracking sounds. Probably just a few bones.

"Here's your present," Colin said. He shoved a package in my face. It had pink and yellow gift wrapping on it. "Go ahead. Open it now," Colin said. "I think your friends want to see it."

Uh-oh.

"I'll open it later," I said, trying to push it out of sight.

"Open it! Open it!" the Wilbur brothers started to chant.

"Colin, don't tease your brother on his birthday," Mom called from the dining room.

"I'm not," Colin shouted. "I'm giving him a present. Here. I'll open it for you."

He raised the package high and ripped off the wrapping paper. Then he held up the gift.

A pair of my underpants. They were dirty. He'd probably taken them from the laundry basket downstairs.

"Hope they fit," Colin said, holding them up so everyone could get a good view. "Here. Let's see if they fit." He pulled the underpants down over my head.

Big laughter.

I mean, *everyone* thought that was just a riot.

Max Doyle, standing there on his twelfth birthday in front of his whole class with a pair of dirty underpants pulled over his head.

Ha, ha.

Well, wasn't this the greatest birthday party ever?

Not.

I wanted to disappear. I wanted to slip through a crack in the floor and never be seen again. I wanted to evaporate. To become that pebbly stuff on the floor of the ocean that bottom-feeders eat.

This had to be the worst birthday party in the history of birthday parties.

But guess what?

A few minutes later, things got worse.

Much worse.

17

"**THIS PARTY IS** *so* not happening," I heard Ashley whisper to some of her friends.

"When does the party actually start?" another kid said. "I mean, like, is this *it*?"

Billy and Willy Wilbur were tossing a couch pillow back and forth across the room. I knew they were getting ready to break something else.

"Someone should let that big dog in again," Marci said. "That was kinda fun."

I rubbed my swollen ankle. I knew the party wasn't going well.

I thought about Quentin upstairs in my room, practicing magic tricks. Maybe it was time to perform. Maybe our awesome tricks would turn things around.

But before I could call Quentin down, Mom started shouting for everyone to come into the dining room. "Birthday cake time! Come on, everyone. Let's sing to Max."

She had set the tall cake with white frosting in the middle of the dining room table. "Max Is 12" was written across the cake in red icing. The candles were all lit.

The kids piled around the table. Billy Wilbur burped really loudly. His brother laughed, but no one else did. The cool kids stayed down at the far end, away from everyone else. One of them was actually reading a book.

Mom started singing, and most everyone joined in. The Wilbur brothers thought it was funny to sing the words late, after everyone had already sung them.

I wanted to get this part over with. It was embarrassing to have everyone stand there and sing that dopey song to me.

I glanced around the table. Where was Quentin? Someone should have called him down for the cake and singing.

"Go ahead, Maxie. Make a wish," Mom said. She gave me a gentle push toward the cake and candles.

I shut my eyes and made a wish. I wished for this party to go from *worst* to *first*. I wished for it all to turn around and become the most awesome party anyone could ever remember.

I opened my eyes. I leaned down to blow out the candles.

And someone else blew them out.

I spun around. I thought Billy and Willy had done it. But they were too far away.

"I'll close the window," Mom said. "There must be a draft."

She pushed down the window. Then she started to light the candles again one by one.

"This is so boring," I heard someone whisper.

"Can't we just eat it?" a boy asked.

Mom shook her head. "Max has to blow out the candles."

It seemed like an hour later, but she finally got them all lit again. And again, I leaned down to blow them out—and the flames disappeared as if someone else had blown on them.

"Ha, ha. Trick candles!" someone yelled.

But I knew better. I knew it had to be Nicky and Tara. It was about time for them to start messing things up.

Everything else had gone wrong so far. Now it was their turn.

"I know you're here!" I shouted. "You're not funny!"

The room grew silent.

"Max, who were you talking to?" Mom asked.

I shrugged. "No one, really."

She frowned at me. "Why don't you go find your friend Quentin and put on your show for everyone while I get the food ready?"

"Excellent!" I said. I turned to all the kids. "Hey, everyone. Quentin and I have been practicing for weeks! We have an awesome show planned."

"Everybody sit down in the living room and get comfortable," Mom said.

"I'll be right back," I said. I climbed the stairs two at a time. My chest started to feel a little fluttery. I was excited. Finally, Quentin and I would be able to show off our juggling and our magic.

"Hey, Quentin!" I called. "Quentin? It's showtime!"

I burst into my room. "Quentin? It's time to—"

I glanced quickly around the room. He wasn't there. I didn't see his magic kit either.

"Hey, Quentin?" My voice came out high and shrill.

I checked the bathroom across the hall. Not there.

Had he decided to practice in Colin's room? I made my way down the hall, but stopped in front of my brother's closed door.

Loud rap music blared from inside. Colin was in his room. No way would Quentin practice there.

So where was he?

"Quentin? Hey, Quentin!" I shouted at the top of my lungs.

I ran back into my room. I glanced all around again.

Whoa. A sheet of white paper on my bed-spread.

What was that? A note?

Yes. A handwritten note. Addressed to me.

I picked it up with a trembling hand. What was *this* about?

Dear Max,

I'm sorry. I just couldn't do it.

I'm not who you think I am.

I'm really sorry.

I had to leave.

Q

18

THE NOTE FELL FROM my hand and fluttered to the floor. But I could still see those handwritten words in my mind.

My brain did flip-flops. I rubbed my temples to stop my throbbing pulse.

What did it mean?

Why did Quentin say he wasn't who I thought he was?

Who *was* he? And why did he run out just before our performance?

The questions were giving me a headache. I picked up the note and, holding it in my trembling hands, read it one more time.

I'm sorry. I just couldn't do it.

Do *what*? It was a terrible mystery.

I wanted to phone Quentin and tell him to come back and explain. But I realized I didn't have a phone number for him.

What exactly did I know about Quentin?

Not very much. I knew that he lived in a big mansion behind a tall hedge. And that he liked to build things and perform magic.

That was about all.

"Hey, Max—where are you?" my mom shouted from downstairs. "Max? Everyone is waiting."

I set Quentin's note down on my bedspread with a loud sigh. *Great* birthday party this was turning out to be. A total bomb.

Traci Wayne hadn't even shown up. I was glad. I didn't want her to see what a loser I was.

Oh, well. The show must go on.

I crossed the room to pick up my duckpins. I cradled them in one arm, then picked up my magic kit.

I stopped at the window and peered out. The sun had dropped behind the trees. It was gray and kind of foggy outside.

But in the dim light, I could see the boy in black. He sat on the ground, leaning against a tree trunk. His face was raised to my house. He was staring up at my bedroom window.

Watching. Watching.

I wanted to open the window and scream at the top of my lungs for him to go away. Get lost—and never come back.

No time for that. I could hear the kids clapping slowly downstairs. Clapping for the show to start.

I spun away from the window. Glanced at Quentin's note one more time. Then turned and headed down to the living room to start my show.

19

"**HERE HE IS, THE** Amazing Max!" Mom shouted as I stepped into the living room.

A duckpin fell out of my arm and hit me on the foot. "Ow!" I cried out in pain and dropped the other two duckpins.

Everyone laughed.

Good start, huh?

"My partner has vanished into thin air," I announced. "But the show will go on without him."

I placed my magic kit on the card table I'd set up in front of the fireplace. I pulled out the magic wand and some other supplies.

I had a trick top hat on the table with a live rabbit hidden inside its secret compartment. And a milk bottle that appeared to empty when you poured it, even though it stayed full.

I was just about ready to start. The room grew quiet.

Most of the kids sat on the floor in front of the card table. The Wilbur brothers were squeezed into an armchair. Willy bumped Billy off, onto the floor. Billy got back into the chair and tried to bump his brother off. Marci and Ashley stood against the far wall, whispering to each other.

"Good evening, everyone. Prepare to be amazed!" I shouted in my deep magician's voice. "First I will show you the magic of the juggler's art."

I cranked up my juggling music on the CD player. Then I took two duckpins, waited for the rhythm to kick in, and started to toss them from hand to hand.

"It's all in the wrist!" I declared. I tossed the pins higher. I had the rhythm. It felt good.

The kids were watching intently now. Even Marci and Ashley had stopped talking and were watching the show.

"And now let's make it a little harder!" I exclaimed. I picked up the third duckpin and added it to the mix.

Three is a lot trickier than two. It means you have to keep one in the air at all times. Your hands have to move really fast. There's no time for any kind of slipup.

But today I was really in the zone! The pins were moving just where I wanted them. Grab and toss. Grab and toss. I grooved with the music and kept the three pins spinning in front of me.

And then it all went crazy.

The pins flew out of my hands. Flew out over the audience as if I had flung them.

"Ohh!" Billy Wilbur uttered a cry as one of the pins thudded into his chest.

I stood and watched in horror as another pin soared across the room. It made a horrible *thunk* as it crashed into Marci's forehead.

She let out a groan, raised her hand to her head, and collapsed to the floor.

"You killed her! You *killed* her!" Ashley screamed.

20

"**MY HEAD. OHH, MY** head," Marci groaned from the floor.

Ashley dropped beside her. "Okay. Erase that. You *didn't* kill her," she shouted. "But she's going to have a big bump on her head."

"I'll sue you!" Marci croaked. "I'll sue!"

I let out a sigh.

Billy Wilbur was holding his chest and gasping for breath. The pin had knocked the wind out of him.

"You did that deliberately!" Willy Wilbur shouted. He ran across the room and dove over the card table. He grabbed me around the waist and tackled me to the floor.

"Get off me!" I shouted, trying to squirm away. "Get off!"

He landed several gut punches before a bunch of kids pulled him away.

"I'll sue!" Marci screamed. She was standing up now and rubbing her forehead. A red lump had swollen to about the size of a tennis ball.

"I'll sue!" She shook her fist at me.

Ashley started to help her out of the house.

"No, wait!" I cried. "Don't miss the best part of the show! I have some great tricks. Really."

The two girls disappeared out the front door. The door slammed behind them.

"Don't you want your party bags?" I called weakly.

Too late.

"Settle down, guys," I said, turning back to the rest of the kids. I motioned for everyone to sit down again. "Accidents happen, you know."

"It wasn't an accident!" Billy Wilbur shouted. "You're dead meat, Max."

"Yeah," his brother chimed in. "Happy birthday, Dead Meat!"

Nice guys.

Of course I knew it wasn't an accident. My hands hadn't slipped while I was juggling. I knew that Nicky and Tara had sent those pins flying.

They probably didn't mean to hit anyone. They just wanted to mess up my juggling, the way they'd messed up my birthday candle blowing.

Would they try to mess up my magic, too?

I'd been looking forward to this day for so long. Looking forward to the party and to performing my tricks.

And so far, it had been a total disaster.

Quentin had disappeared. The creepy ghost-boy in black was still outside, waiting for I-don't-know-what. One of the cool kids I'd wanted to impress had a major lump on her head and had to leave. Traci Wayne had never even shown up. . . .

The list of horrors went on and on.

And there were Nicky and Tara. So angry at me, they were trying to ruin my party.

Okay, I made a mistake. I shouldn't have told them to stay away. But I never dreamed they'd be this mean.

Well . . . I'm a brave guy. I stepped up to the table and started my show.

First I performed a few easy card tricks.

The tricks went well. The cards didn't fly out of my hands and hit people in the eye or anything.

I did a few tricks with the wand. Whipped the wand into the air, and it turned into a bouquet of flowers.

No problem. Worked perfectly.

A few kids clapped. I was starting to win them back. Time to do one of the harder tricks.

"Okay, everyone! Take a look inside this top hat," I said. I held up the hat so they could see inside it.

"As you can all see, it's totally empty."

I moved it in front of them slowly so they all could see.

Then I set the hat back down on the table.

"The eyes can be deceived!" I said. "Sometimes a great magician can make something appear where there was nothing! Watch carefully!"

Slowly, I waved my wand back and forth over the hat.

"Come to life!" I cried. "Come to life!"

I reached a hand inside the hat. I snapped open the secret compartment.

Then I lowered both hands to lift out the bunny rabbit.

My fingers curled around something thin and crackly. I heard a high screech from inside the hat. Something scratched my palm. And then fluttered up between my hands.

And I opened my mouth in a horrified scream.

21

THE FIRST BAT FLEW out of the hat, screeching, its red eyes flaring. It soared up to the ceiling and then shot across the room.

Kids started shouting and ducking.

The second bat fluttered out silently. It hovered in front of my face for a few seconds, then turned and swooped forward—and landed on a girl's shoulder.

She screamed and slapped it away.

Flapping its wings hard, the bat hopped onto her head and let out a screech.

She slapped at it frantically, swatting it off with both hands.

The first bat came swooping down over the birthday cake in the dining room. Then it flew back into the living room, dropping low, and shot into a boy's chest.

The boy let out a choked cry. The bat bounced off him and onto the lap of the girl beside him.

"Open the front door!" I shouted. "Somebody—open the door!"

My mom was already there. She swung the door open. Some kids ran to the front window and hoisted it up all the way.

Kids were running and screaming and ducking and covering their heads as the bats swooped down at them.

Your typical birthday party.

If you have two ghosts who want to teach you a lesson.

Finally, the two bats turned and darted out the front door, side by side. Mom slammed the door behind them.

I saw Colin on the bottom stair, leaning on the banister. He had a big grin on his face. "Nice trick, Maxie," he said. "Do another one."

"No—please! No more tricks!" Mom cried.

"No more tricks! No more tricks!" Billy and Willy and some other kids started to chant. "No more tricks! No more tricks!"

"Okay, okay," I muttered. I slammed my magic case shut.

"Is the party over?" a boy shouted.

"Can we go now?" a girl asked.

"Yes. Can we go?"

Well, score another success for Max, I thought. Kids are *begging* to leave.

Awesome party.

"Are you satisfied?" I screamed at Nicky and

Tara. I couldn't see them, but I knew they had to be there. "Are you happy now?"

Kids stared at me.

"Max, are you okay?" Mom called, hurrying over. "Did one of those bats bite you?"

"I'm fine," I said. "Just fine."

"He's rabid," Colin called. "Look out, everyone. Maxie is rabid!" Laughing, he went back up to his room.

I wanted to save the party. I didn't want everyone to go home now and tell their parents it was the worst day of their lives—and they'd been attacked by bats.

"Wait. We're going to play Twister!" I shouted. "Come on, guys. I've got two Twister mats. Double Twister! Come on. Let's do it. I've got prizes for the winners!"

Some kids were halfway to the door. But they stopped when I said the word "prizes."

"What kinds of prizes?" Willy Wilbur asked.

I had to think fast. I didn't really have any prizes. "Uh . . . some new PlayStation games," I said. Colin had every PlayStation game ever made. I could probably sneak some from his shelves.

A few minutes later, everyone was playing Twister.

I had two mats. We cleared away the furniture,

and I spread them out side by side in the living room.

The game was funny. Kids were climbing all over each other. Lots of laughing and groaning and joking.

Then suddenly, the room grew silent.

"I . . . can't move," a girl said. She was on her hands and knees on the mat.

"Whoa. Weird. I'm stuck here, too," another girl said from down on the floor.

"Hey, what's up with this?" a boy cried.

I gazed around the room in horror. My friends had all frozen in place, as if they were locked in a photograph.

"Max—help me up!" a boy shouted.

"You're joking about this, right?" Billy Wilbur said. He was flat on his back between the mats. I watched him struggle and strain to sit up.

"My back is *glued* to the floor!" he wailed.

"I'm stuck to Sarah!" a girl named Susan shrieked. "Help us! We're totally stuck together!"

"My shoes are glued to the rug! I can't move!" someone cried.

I looked for my mom. I didn't see her.

Kids were struggling and straining, grunting and groaning as they tried to stand up. A boy under a pile of kids started to cry. Other kids began screaming.

"Let us up! Let us up!"

"Help me! I can't move!"

"We're all glued together!"

Frozen in horror and disbelief, I stared at my friends as they screamed and struggled, unable to move. Finally, I shook off my fright.

I reached down to pull a boy up—and realized I couldn't move either.

My feet were glued to the floor!

22

I MADE A GRAB for my friend's hand. Missed. And fell facedown onto the carpet.

I struggled to pull myself up.

But now my hands and knees were glued down.

"Help us!"

"Somebody call 911!"

"This is totally impossible!"

"Max, is this one of your stupid magic tricks?"

The cries and shouts rang against the walls as kids pulled and twisted themselves, pushed and strained. But no one could move.

It wasn't one of *my* tricks, I knew.

It had to be one of Nicky and Tara's.

"Nicky! Tara! Let everyone go!" I shouted. "I'm sorry! Do you hear me? I'm sorry! I should have invited you!"

A hush fell over the room.

"Max? Who are you talking to?" the girl named Susan asked.

96

"Nicky? Tara?" I cried. "I know you can hear me!"

"Max, you're freaking us out!" Susan said. "There's no one here named Nicky or Tara."

"Good trick, Max," Willy Wilbur said. "You got us all scared. Now let us up. I'm warning you, dude."

"Yeah. I'm warning you too," his brother added. "If I could raise my fists off the floor, I'd be pounding you with them."

"Tara? Is this one of your spells?" I called out.

I struggled to lift my right hand off the carpet. But it wouldn't budge.

"Tara? Did you get this spell from that old spell book you have?" I cried. "This isn't funny. We're not enjoying this."

No reply.

"You've gone too far this time!" I shouted.

"Max, we know you're not talking to anyone real," Sarah said. "Please—stop the magic trick and let us up."

"Yeah. We're all impressed," Willy Wilbur said. "But let us up so we can punch out your lights."

"This is the worst party I've ever gone to," I heard someone mutter.

"Worst party in *history*," someone else whispered.

"We're gonna *get* you for this," Billy Wilbur growled.

I ignored them and called out to Nicky and Tara again. "I'm sorry!" I shouted. "Did you hear me? I've apologized six times. So stop this! Let my friends get up!"

I let out a gasp as Nicky and Tara suddenly appeared in the doorway. They both stood awkwardly, jerking their arms around as if trying to balance.

"We just got here, Max," Tara said.

"And we're frozen too!" Nicky exclaimed.

"I'm glued to the floor!" Tara wailed. "It's not us, Max!"

"Who is *doing* this?" Nicky cried.

I heard a sound behind me. A crackling sound. Some short pops.

I turned—just in time to see the birthday cake explode.

23

EVERYONE SCREAMED AT ONCE.

The cake blew up with a deafening roar. Chunks of white and chocolate cake shot across the room. They splattered the walls and ceiling and dropped onto my friends.

A thick glob of chocolate icing slopped into Willy Wilbur's face and dripped down his shirt. Kids were sputtering and shouting.

And suddenly, they were on their feet.

I saw kids stand up and stretch and help other kids up to test their arms and legs.

Kids were checking out their hands. Making sure their knees worked.

I lurched forward, startled that I could walk again. My shoes slid in a puddle of chocolate icing. I grabbed the back of a chair to keep my balance.

I helped Susan and Sarah to their feet. Then I turned and saw the smoke shooting up from the remains of the cake.

A column of thick black smoke hissed up to the ceiling.

Kids were running now. Pushing each other, stampeding for the front door.

I stood and watched the smoke as it divided in two. It hissed and crackled, billowing off the ceiling. Two waves of smoke now, floating over my head.

Swirling, crackling, the smoke lowered itself over me. And I saw two figures form, like dark clouds.

The two dark-winged creatures sailed up, just beneath the ceiling, like the shadow bats you make with your hands. Just like those bats— except ten times as big.

My mouth dropped open in horror. My breath caught in my throat.

I stared up at these two bats, formed from the smoke of the cake explosion. I stared up at them, trembling as they circled me slowly.

The two shadow bats circled me, round and round—till I shut my eyes from dizziness. And over the whistle and hiss of the flying smoke creatures, I heard Nicky and Tara calling to me.

"Shades!" I heard Nicky scream, his voice high and shrill with terror.

"Max, they are *shades*!" Tara cried. "Not human, not ghost! Shades from the underworld!"

"The shades are the ones making all the problems!" Nicky called. "They did it all. They ruined your party."

With a rush of hot wind, the two shades swooped in on me, covering me in smoke. Smothering me.

I started to cough. I couldn't breathe.

"Help me!" I cried to Nicky and Tara. "Do something!"

I couldn't hear a reply.

The twin smoke bats wrapped themselves around me, covering me in a hot, choking darkness.

I shielded my face with my arms, trying to protect myself. I struggled to breathe. My throat and chest burned with each breath.

Sputtering, coughing, I felt myself rising from the floor.

"Help! Put me down!" I gasped.

They were carrying me, lifting me off the floor and sweeping me away.

"Nicky! Tara!"

I tried to call to my friends. But my words were swallowed by the thick, steaming smoke.

I was moving fast now. Being swept away.

I couldn't see.

I couldn't breathe.

Where were they taking me?

What did they want with me?

24

LIKE FLOATING IN A dream, I thought.

Floating blindly, not asleep.

But not awake, either.

I had the terrifying thought that I was going to float like this forever, inside a heavy black cloud.

Float without seeing, without breathing, without *being anywhere*.

Was I still alive? Or had the bats smothered me to death?

The burning pain in my throat, my nostrils, my chest told me I was still alive. My hacking coughs and loud, wheezing breaths told me I was still alive.

But how long would these two shades hold me in their smoky grip?

How long would I float, helpless, like this?

The question was answered quickly.

I landed hard on both feet. My body was jarred as pain shot up my legs and back, to my shoulders.

"Owww. Oh, help."

I stumbled forward into the smoke.

And the haze started to lift. Slowly, the black turned to gray. And then I could see the faint image of tiles on a wall in front of me.

Resting my hands on my knees, I bent forward and concentrated on breathing. I took a long, cool breath, then slowly let it out.

Then another.

The dizziness started to fade. I watched the two shades drift away from me.

They whirled low over my head, tangling together. Two smoke bats hissing as they darted back and forth above me.

And then they rose up high, twisting round and round each other—and vanished through the yellow tile wall.

Still breathing hard, I stared at the wall. I waited for them to come shooting back.

But . . . no sign of them.

Trembling, I spun around. Where was I? Where had they carried me?

My teeth were chattering. I tightened my jaw hard, trying to stop them.

Bright white moonlight poured through a long window. The light shimmered off the high ceiling and sparkled in front of me.

In the water.

Water?

I shook my head, trying to clear it.

And I finally recognized where I was standing.

The new swimming pool at school. The swimming pool that I'd helped to dedicate just a few months before.

I was standing at the edge of the pool. With a gasp, I stumbled back until I was pressed against the wall.

No lights were on. The moonlight shimmering in the pool made the only light. The water splashed softly, lapping against the sides of the pool.

Why did the shades bring me here?

I slid down to the floor and sat cross-legged on the cool tiles. I took deep breaths, inhaling the sharp chlorine smell, and tried to calm myself down.

Tried to think clearly.

Why am I here? Why?

Nothing I thought about made any sense. I stared at the sparkling lights dancing on the water. And I shivered.

Then I heard a sharp cough.

Footsteps clicking on the tiles. I wasn't alone.

Feeling my whole body tense, I jumped to my feet.

"Who—who's there?" My question came out in a choked whisper.

I gasped when I recognized the short, chubby figure who stepped out of the shadows.

Mayor Stank!

He came walking toward me quickly along the edge of the pool, shoes clicking on the hard floor. He wore a gray business suit with a bright yellow necktie.

He had a wide grin on his face. His bald head reflected the twinkling moonlight, making him look all silvery and strange.

"Remember me, Max?" he called. His voice echoed hollowly off the walls.

"Why—y-yes," I stammered, pressing myself against the wall to stop my trembling.

He stopped a few feet from me. His eyes glowed brightly. His grin grew wider. "Remember me, Max? Mayor Stank? Remember? You pushed me into the pool? On TV? In front of the whole town? Remember?"

I just nodded. I couldn't speak.

"Well, I don't forget things, Max," he said, lowering his voice to a growl. "It's payback time."

25

HE MOVED CLOSER. Close enough for me to see the beads of sweat glistening on his forehead and on his bald head. He kept working his jaw, as if he had a wad of chewing gum in his mouth.

His tiny black eyes were locked on mine.

I pressed myself tightly against the cool wall. The lights danced in front of me. I wanted to shut my eyes, but I knew I couldn't.

I knew I was in major trouble here.

I broke the staring battle. I looked away. Turned my gaze to the gently lapping water.

"Go ahead. Jump in," he whispered.

"Excuse me?" I blurted out. "Mayor Stank, I—"

"Jump in, Max. Go ahead."

I took a few steps away from him. I wondered if I could just turn and run.

Was the door open? Could I escape through the exit, or did he have it blocked off somehow?

Were those two shades waiting for me on the other side of the door?

My legs were shaking too hard to run.

My heart pounded so hard, my chest ached. And I could feel my pulse pounding in my eardrums.

Was he *crazy*? Why had he brought me here? To jump in the pool?

"I'm a fair man, Max," he said, keeping his steely gaze on me. "But I have no choice. I have to pay you back."

"Wh-why?" I choked out.

He ignored my question. "Go ahead. Jump in the pool," he said, working his jaw angrily. "Do two hundred laps, and we'll call it even."

"Huh?" I gasped. "I . . . I'm not a good swimmer. I *sink*. I can't do two hundred laps on dry land!"

"Funny," he growled. "But I'm not joking. Do two hundred laps, Max. Stop stalling. Do it. Now."

"I can't do two hundred," I said in a shaky voice. "How about five? A compromise? What do you say? Five?"

He scowled at me. "Don't make me laugh so hard. You'll give me wrinkles."

"I—I'm serious," I stammered. "I can't—"

"You're going in the water, Max," he said softly. "You can come out when you've done two hundred laps."

"But—but—" I sputtered. "My skin! I'll get all

107

pruney. How will that look for my class pictures on Monday?"

"I'm a fair man," he said again. He wiped sweat off his bald head with the palm of his hand. "You pushed me in the pool. You made a fool of me. Now I just want us to be even."

"You're crazy! You can't do this!" I cried, balling my hands into tight fists. I felt my anger start to burn my chest. "I don't care if you're the mayor! You can't force me to swim laps!"

Mayor Stank let out a long sigh. He raised his eyes and peered over my shoulder. "Quentin," he said, "push your friend Max into the water."

I turned and saw Quentin step out from the shadows.

"Push him in," Mayor Stank ordered.

Quentin hesitated for a long moment. Then he said, "Okay, Dad."

26

HUH? DAD?

Did he say *Dad*?

Quentin grabbed my shoulder. He gave me a gentle push toward the edge of the pool.

His blond hair caught the moonlight from the window and made his face glow. I saw his chin tremble. He kept his eyes on the pool. He wouldn't look at me.

"I'm sorry, Max," he whispered. "I have to do what my dad says."

He pushed me forward until I was just inches from the water. I spun around to face him. He still wouldn't look me in the eye.

"Your dad is the mayor?" I said. "You never told me."

"Quentin, get a move on. Stop stalling," Mayor Stank called. Again, he wiped sweat off his bald head with one hand. "Let's get the Max Olympics started."

Quentin had both hands on my shoulders. I tried to push back, but he was surprisingly strong.

He lowered his head so that his dad wouldn't see him talk to me. "I wanted to be your friend," he whispered. "But Dad wouldn't let me. He forced me to spy on you. He forced me to get you here."

My heels poked over the edge of the pool. "Don't I even get to undress?" I called to Mayor Stank. "How about I go home and get my swim trunks?"

"You pushed me in when I was wearing my best suit," he replied. "I'm just trying to be fair, Max. You can't criticize me for trying to be fair, can you?"

"It's hard to say what's fair and what's not fair," I said. "Maybe we should sit down somewhere. You know. In a nice, dry place. And talk about it."

"Nice try," the mayor said, narrowing his tiny eyes at me.

"He made me do everything," Quentin whispered. "I had found an old spell book in your house. He made me use a spell from it to call up those two shades. I was so frightened."

"Me too," I muttered.

"I'm really sorry I messed up your party," Quentin said.

I gazed over my shoulder at the sparkling water.

"No way can I swim all those laps," I told Quentin.

"My dad really holds a grudge," Quentin whispered. "It's one of his biggest faults."

"What are you two yakking about?" Mayor Stank cried angrily. "Shut up and push him in. Then I've got a good job for you, Quentin. You can be the official scorekeeper. You get to count the laps."

"That'll be an easy job," I muttered. "You only have to count to three or four. And then you can watch me *drown*!"

"I'm really sorry, Max," Quentin whispered. "I hope you'll accept my apology."

He spun me around and gave me a hard push.

I searched for my ghost friends. "Nicky? Tara?" I shouted. "Are you here? Help me!"

27

"Nicky? Tara?"

My voice echoed off the tile walls.

I shut my eyes, praying to hear their voices. But no. The only sound was my harsh breathing and the soft splash of the water in front of me.

"Nicky? Tara?"

"That's an old trick!" Mayor Stank shouted. "You're trying to make me think someone else is here. I'm smarter than that, Max. I'm the mayor. I didn't get the job by being dumb."

I had to stall. I had to think of a way to escape. "Uh . . . my dad voted for you!" I called.

"I met your dad once," Mayor Stank said. "He's a jerk."

Quentin tightened his grip on my arms. I was seconds away from drowning time.

"Go ahead, Quentin," the mayor said, motioning with both hands. "One more push. Time for the entertainment to start."

He narrowed his eyes at me. "I'm sure you

understand, Max. I don't want to hurt you. I just want to get even."

"Sorry," Quentin whispered one more time.

He pushed me forward.

The water rose up in front of me.

And in that instant, I had an idea. An idea to rescue myself.

It was a crazy idea. Totally insane.

No way could it possibly work . . .

28

I TWISTED MY BODY. Spun around to face Quentin. Raised my hands—and dug them into his armpits.

I remembered that afternoon in my room when Colin had started to tickle me. He'd tickled me until I screamed. And when we looked across the room, Quentin had frozen.

Quentin had gone into some kind of trance.

Later, he said he had a strange reaction to tickling. He just couldn't *stand* it. It always put him in a weird frozen state.

As Quentin shoved me toward the pool, I remembered that afternoon. And I thought, Maybe . . . Maybe like son, like father.

Would Quentin's dad have the same strange reaction to tickling?

I dug my fingers hard into Quentin's armpits. "Tickle! Tickle!" I screamed. "Are you ticklish?"

"Stop!" Quentin cried, twisting and squirming, frantic to escape.

I lowered my hands to his ribs and tickled hard. "Tickle, tickle! Who's ticklish?"

"Stop. . . . Oh . . . oh . . ." Quentin fell backward, kicking his legs in the air. Helpless. Like a turtle on its back.

I dug my fingers into his ribs. Into his belly.

"Stop . . . Please—Max!"

I tickled harder. Tickled his ribs, his stomach, his armpits.

Quentin froze. Eyes wide open. His whole body just went stiff.

He was in that strange trance again.

Gasping for breath, I jumped to my feet. And turned to the mayor.

Was it working? Did Mayor Stank have the same weird reaction as his son?

Yes!

My heart pounding, I saw him standing stiffly in place. His mouth hung open, twisted as if *he* was the one being tickled. His eyes were bulging. His hands were at his sides, balled into tight fists.

He didn't move. He was in the ticklish trance.

I took a deep shuddering breath. And stepped back a few paces from the pool edge.

And as I did, I saw the mayor stagger forward. Mouth frozen open, eyes bulging without blinking. In his trance, the mayor stumbled—and toppled into the pool with a loud, echoing splash.

29

QUENTIN DIDN'T MOVE. He lay on his back with both legs in the air, staring up at the ceiling.

I stepped over him and walked to where Mayor Stank had fallen in. I heard him splashing and thrashing, and I saw water wash up onto the tile floor.

"Help me!" the mayor screamed.

The cold water must have snapped him out of his trance.

"Help me, Max! I can't swim!"

I got down on my knees, leaned over the side, and stretched out my hand. The mayor tried to reach it, but he sank below the surface, then popped back up, coughing and choking and sputtering.

His pudgy fingers slapped at the water. His bright yellow necktie floated up over his face, and he frantically swiped it away.

"Help me! Don't just sit there watching!" he screamed.

"I'm trying to help you!" I shouted.

He sputtered and coughed some more. And sank under the water for a few seconds.

"My shoes! My shoes are weighing me down!" he cried when he came back up. "Help me, Max!"

I reached as far as I could and grabbed his soaked suit jacket with both hands. He started to sink and almost pulled me in with him.

"Grab my hands!" I shouted.

He raised his hands, and I wrapped my fingers around them. But he slipped out of my grasp. Once. Twice.

I grabbed again and again.

Finally, I tightened my hands around his wrists and got him to the side. Then I tugged him up by his necktie. And heaved him onto the floor.

He plopped onto his stomach like a beached whale, and about a quart of water poured from his mouth. "Unnnnnngggh." He made a horrible groaning, barfing sound. And rolled onto his back.

I turned and saw that Quentin had returned to life. He bent over the mayor. "Are you okay, Dad?" he asked, grabbing his dad's hand.

Mayor Stank groaned again. He let Quentin pull him up to a sitting position. Then more pool water drooled down his chin.

"Dad? Are you okay? Dad?" Quentin kept repeating.

Finally, the mayor struggled to his feet. Water

poured from his suit. He took a few steps. His shoes squished against the floor.

"I'm okay," he muttered to Quentin.

Then he turned to me. "I think we're even," he said. "I'm an honest man. Yes, I may be insane. Because I have to have my revenge, even against a twelve-year-old boy. But I'm honest. And when I say we're even, we're even."

He grabbed Quentin's arm. "Let's get out of here."

Quentin turned to me. "I'm sorry, Max. He made me do it."

I watched them hurry out of the building. The doors slammed behind them. I couldn't stop shivering. A close call.

The mayor was totally insane. He'd wanted me to swim two hundred laps!

I hugged myself and tried to stop shivering. The pool shimmered in front of me. Moonlight washed through the tall windows.

Mom and Dad must wonder where I am, I thought. If I told them the truth, they'd never believe me.

I took a deep breath and strode down the side of the pool, pushed open the door, and made my way outside.

As I started to walk home, I felt bad, really bad. This was supposed to be an awesome birthday. Instead, it was horrible in every way.

My party was a major flop. I'd embarrassed myself in front of all the cool kids and my whole class. And I'd lost a friend. At least, someone I *thought* was a friend.

I turned the corner onto Bleek Street. My house was on the next block. I was walking with my head down, thinking hard, feeling sorry for myself, not seeing anything.

Suddenly, I realized I wasn't alone.

I turned, focused my eyes—and saw the boy in black. Behind a tall driveway stone. Watching me.

Watching me . . .

I couldn't take it anymore.

I let out a scream. I leaped across the driveway and grabbed the boy by the throat.

"What do you want?" I screamed, shaking him. "Tell me! *Why are you watching me?*"

30

HIS EYES BULGED. He let out a choked groan.

I realized I was choking him. I let go of his neck and dropped my hands.

"Tell me," I said. "Tell me what you are doing."

He rubbed his throat. He had a boy's face, but old eyes. Old and tired, with deep wrinkles underneath.

"It's my job," he said. "I'm doing my job."

I stared at him.

A breeze made the leaves in the trees tremble. The moon disappeared behind a wall of clouds. Darkness spread around us.

"I don't understand," I said. "Explain yourself. What is your job?"

"I was hired to watch you," he said. I waited for him to say more. But he just stared at me, breathing hard.

"Why?" I asked. "Come on. Explain it. I'm just a kid. Why on earth would someone hire you to watch me?"

He blinked. "Aren't you Max Boyle?"

"Excuse me?" It was my turn to blink. "Max *who*?"

"Aren't you Max Boyle?" he asked, staring hard at me. "Aren't you haunted by three evil ghosts—Larry, Mary, and Maurice? They plan to kill you!"

My mouth dropped open. It took me a long time to find my voice.

"Dude, you've made a big mistake," I said finally.

He squinted at me. "Mistake?"

"I'm not Max Boyle," I said. "I'm Max *Doyle*. And I'm not haunted by three ghosts named Larry, Mary, and Maurice."

"Oh, wow!" The boy let out a cry and slapped his forehead. "Oh, wow. Oh, wow. I'm totally embarrassed. I've been watching the *wrong house*!"

He slapped his forehead again. "This is a major goof-up," he said. "I'm going to lose my job. I blew it. I totally blew it!"

"I . . . I hope Max Boyle is okay," I said.

"Goodbye and good luck," he said. He gave me a quick wave, turned, and vanished into the trees, muttering to himself.

I stood there for a moment, staring into the darkness. The moon appeared again, and its light washed over the ground.

"That solves that mystery," I said to myself.

When I got home, I found Nicky and Tara waiting for me in my room. Nicky was playing with my Game Boy. Tara had a book in her lap.

She dropped it when she saw me and came rushing over. "Max, where were you? Nicky and I were worried."

"I was at the swimming pool," I said. "I thought maybe you'd be there to help me."

"Swimming pool?" Nicky said, putting down the Game Boy. "Isn't this a weird time to go for a swim?"

I sighed. "You were right about Quentin," I told them. "He's a bad dude."

I told them the whole story about Mayor Stank and about how Quentin was his son and how they'd wanted to make me swim two hundred laps at the new swimming pool.

They listened quietly, shaking their heads and *tsk-tsk*ing.

"I hope you learned your lesson," Tara said when I finished. "You should always listen to us."

"Yeah," Nicky agreed. "You know, your party was a total flop because we weren't there."

"I'm sorry," I said. "I was totally wrong. I should have invited you. I lost my temper, and I was wrong."

Tara grinned. "Go on apologizing, Max. I like it."

So I apologized some more.

I apologized until my phone rang.

It was nearly midnight. Who would be calling so late at night?

I picked it up and heard Traci's voice. "Max? When is your party?" she asked. "I forgot to write it down. Is it this week or next?"

TO BE CONTINUED

ABOUT THE AUTHOR

Robert Lawrence Stine's scary stories have made him one of the bestselling children's authors in history. "Kids like to be scared!" he says, and he has proved it by selling more than 300 million books. R.L. teamed up with Parachute Press to create Fear Street, the first and number one bestselling young adult horror series. He then went on to launch Goosebumps, the creepy bestselling series that gave kids chills all over the world and made him the number one children's author of all time (*The Guinness Book of Records*).

R.L. Stine lives in Manhattan with his wife, Jane, their son, Matthew, and their dog, Nadine. He says he has never seen a ghost—but he's still looking!

Don't miss the next book
in the Mostly Ghostly series,

Freaks and Shrieks!

Wimp or Chimp?

MAX MADE A DEAL WITH Nicky and Tara, the two
ghosts who live in his bedroom: If he helps them
figure out how they got turned into ghosts, they'll
help him prove to his dad that he isn't a worthless
wimp.

Well, Max is about to make good on his end of
the bargain. Someone saw what happened to the
kids. Someone may know the secret that will bring
them back to life! The problem is that the someone
isn't a someone—the someone is a chimpanzee!
And Max is going to switch brains with him to
learn the secret!

WE STARTED DOWN A long white hall. Even the carpet was white. The animal cries became fainter as we turned a corner into another white hall.

Nicky and Tara glanced around nervously. "Did our parents work here?" Tara asked.

Dr. Smollet nodded. He led us into a big, square room filled with computer equipment. The walls were solid white. Bright lights beamed down from the low ceiling.

Dr. Smollet pulled off his raincoat and his suit jacket with it, and tossed them on a chair. He tugged down the sleeves of his starched white shirt.

I could still hear the animal shrieks in the distance. Sad, frightened cries. They made me feel frightened too.

Had we made a big mistake?

I swallowed hard. My mouth was suddenly very dry, and my hands felt as cold as ice. I jammed them into my jeans pockets—and felt the deck of trick cards.

The lab was neat and clean. The monitors blinked silently. The big electronic machines clicked and hummed. Dr. Smollet smiled as the three of us gazed around.

"This lab belonged to your parents," he told Nicky and Tara. "This is where they worked. And I worked here alongside them."

"Wow," Nicky said, shaking his head. He walked up to a long table of laptops. "I think I remember being here. It's a faint memory. But it's coming back to me."

"Yes, I remember all the computers," Tara said. "And all those wires and cables up on the ceiling."

She pulled at her dangling plastic earrings. She always tugged them when she was thinking hard or trying to remember something.

"We were here, Nicky," she said. "I know we were. Why can't I remember it better?"

Dr. Smollet leaned his hands on the table. "That's what we're here to find out," he said.

He pointed to the machines against the wall. "Your parents and I worked here, capturing evil ghosts. Your parents were on a mission. They believed a lot of the evil in the world was caused by these spirits. They found a way to capture them and keep them prisoner here."

Dr. Smollet sighed. "But one evil ghost—a man

named Phears—escaped. I tried to fight him off. But he was too powerful for me. He injured me. He knocked me out. When I came to, *all* the evil ghosts had escaped. Phears had freed them all."

"We—we've run into Phears," Nicky said.

Dr. Smollet's blue eyes grew wide. "You and your sister were here in the lab on that awful day. Don't you remember? Don't you understand?"

Nicky and Tara froze. They stared at him, speechless.

"We . . . didn't know," Tara said finally.

"You were visiting your parents here," Dr. Smollet said. "When Phears escaped, he did something to your family. To all four of you."

"You were here," I said. "Didn't you see what happened to them?"

Dr. Smollet shook his head. "No. I didn't see anything. I was out cold."

He took a deep breath and smoothed back his white hair. "But I have someone here who saw everything," he said. "I have a witness. I told you his name. Mr. Harvey."

"Where is he?" Tara asked.

Nicky strode up beside Dr. Smollet. "Can we talk to him? Is he here now?"

Dr. Smollet nodded. "Mr. Harvey is the only one who saw everything that happened that day.

He saw Phears escape. He saw Phears free the other ghosts. And he saw what Phears did to you and your parents."

The scientist loosened his tie. It was cool in the lab, but beads of sweat rolled down his forehead.

"Mr. Harvey *may* know the secret. He may know how to bring your family back to life," he said, gazing intently at my two ghost friends.

"Please—can we see him?" Tara cried. "Can we talk to him now?"

Dr. Smollet cleared his throat. He tugged at his tie again. "Well . . . there's a small problem. I'll show you."

He swung away from the table and walked quickly out of the lab. The door closed behind him.

Nicky and Tara stared at each other. Then they turned to me.

"I . . . I don't know what to say," Tara confessed. "I'm shaking!"

"Me too," Nicky said, his voice cracking. He pumped his fists in the air. "This is too good to be true. Do you think Mr. Harvey can really bring us back to life? Can he really tell what happened to us?"

The lab door swung open.

Dr. Smollet stepped in, followed by another figure.

"This is Mr. Harvey," Dr. Smollet said.

Tara's mouth dropped open.

Nicky gasped.

I stared hard at Mr. Harvey. My brain felt as if it was spinning in my head. "But . . . but . . . ," I stammered. "Mr. Harvey is a *chimp*!"